515 4393
1-24-79
44

The
Ex-Magician
and Other
Stories

The Ex-Magician and Other Stories

Murilo Rubião

Translated from the Portuguese
by Thomas Colchie

Harper & Row, Publishers
New York, Hagerstown, San Francisco, London

THE EX-MAGICIAN AND OTHER STORIES. English translation copyright © 1979 by Thomas Colchie. All rights reserved. Printed in the United States of America. No part of this book may be used or reproduced in any manner whatsoever without written permission except in the case of brief quotations embodied in critical articles and reviews. For information address Harper & Row, Publishers, Inc., 10 East 53rd Street, New York, N.Y. 10022. Published simultaneously in Canada by Fitzhenry & Whiteside Limited, Toronto.

FIRST EDITION

Designed by Janice Stern

Library of Congress Cataloguing in Publication Data

Rubião, Murilo.
    The ex-magician and other stories.

    I. Title.
PZ4.R8916Ex   [PQ9697.R93]   869'.3   78–2064
ISBN 0–06–013708–8

79 80 81 82 83 10 9 8 7 6 5 4 3 2 1

Contents

They that come after him
shall be astonished at his day,
as they that went before were
affrighted.

Job,XVII:20

The
Ex-Magician
and Other
Stories

The Dragons

I am a brother to dragons,
and a companion to owls.
Job, xxx:29

The first dragons to appear in our city suffered a great deal due to the backwardness of our customs. They received precarious training at best, and their moral instruction was compromised dreadfully by absurd discussions which their arrival had somehow prompted.

Very few of us were able to understand them, and the general confusion was such that, until we saw to their education, we were hopelessly lost in contradictory speculation as to their race and country of origin.

The initial dispute was the fault of the vicar. Convinced that—in spite of their docile, almost pleasant exterior—they were still messengers of the Devil, he refused to allow me to begin to instruct them. Instead, he gave orders to have them confined to an old house, which was to be first exorcised and to which no one was permitted access. By the time he repented of his mistake, the controversy had already widened, with one elderly grammarian denying them the quality of dragons: "an Asiatic thing, of European importation." Another reader of newspapers, a high-school dropout with vaguely scientific ideas, spoke of "an-

1

tediluvian monsters." Still others, making the sign of the cross, suggested headless mules and werewolves.

Only the children, who secretly played with our guests, understood that their new companions were simple dragons. To them, however, no one bothered to listen.

Exhaustion and time overcame the obstinacy of many. Even those who still maintained their convictions at least avoided the subject.

Nevertheless, the polemic resurfaced after a brief respite. The pretext was a suggestion for utilizing dragons as a means of transportation. Everyone agreed that the idea was excellent, but quarreling broke out as to the specific distribution of the animals, whose number was far less than those who hoped to make use of them.

To put an end to the discussion, which threatened to drag on indefinitely and to no practical purpose, the vicar subscribed to the following proposal: the dragons should be baptized, given proper names, and taught to read and write.

Until that moment I had acted with discretion, so as to avoid contributing to the general aggravation of tempers. And if, for an instant, I seemed to lack my usual composure, or proper respect for the good father, I must blame the prevailing foolishness. I was utterly irritated and gave vent to my disapproval:

"They are dragons! They have no need of baptism or any proper names!"

Shocked at my attitude, which normally conformed to that of the community at large, His Reverence gave ample display of his humility by withdrawing the idea of baptism. I returned the gesture, by acceding to his demand for proper names.

I comprehended the extent of my responsibility when, rescued from the neglect they had fallen into, they were finally brought to me for instruction. The majority had contracted various unknown maladies, as a result of which they slowly died. Only two had still survived, unfortunately the most corrupt of the lot. Endowed with even greater cunning than their brothers, they would sneak away from the old mansion at night, to go drinking at a local tavern. Since the bartender enjoyed watching them get tipsy, he didn't charge for the liquor he served. Eventually the identical scene, month after month, ceased to amuse him, and he refused to give them any more drinks. In order to sustain their vice, they decided to resort to petty thefts.

In the meantime, I still clung to the possibility of reeducating them and thereby vindicating the success of my undertaking in the eyes of the incredulous. I took advantage of my friendship with the police commissioner in order to have them released from jail, where they were constantly remanded on the same charges: petty larceny, drunken disorder.

Since I had never taught dragons before, I spent a great deal of time inquiring about their past, their families and pedagogical methods in their own homeland. The successive interrogations to which they were subjected provided me with little information. Particularly since, having come to our city while fairly young, they remembered everything rather confusedly, including the death of their mother, who had fallen off a precipice just after the ascent of the first mountain. And to further complicate my task, the already weak memory of my pupils was beclouded with constant ill-humor, occasioned by poor sleep and continual hangovers.

The ingrained habits of teaching, coupled with a lack of my own offspring, contributed to my eventually bestowing a certain paternal regard upon them. Moreover, a gentle candor that sometimes radiated from their eyes induced me to pardon faults in them which I should never have forgiven in my other students.

Odorico, the oldest of the dragons, caused me the greatest problems. At once disastrously mischievous and completely engaging, he was transported at the mere sight of a skirt. Because of that habit and, even more, out of some inborn tendency toward degeneracy, he was constantly truant from classes. Women somehow found him attractive, and there was one who became so impassioned, she left her husband to go live with him.

I did everything to terminate the sinful alliance, but never managed to separate them. They refused my appeals with a voiceless, impenetrable defiance. My words never reached them: Odorico would smile at Raquel, and, reassured, she would once again bend over the laundry she was washing.

Sometime later they found her crying next to her lover's body. His death was attributed to an accidental shot, probably by some hunter with a poor aim. Her husband, however, told another story.

With the death of Odorico, my wife and I transferred our affections to the last of the dragons. We took upon ourselves his complete rehabilitation and finally managed, after considerable effort, to wean him from alcoholism. Perhaps having a son of our own would not have approached what we accomplished with such loving persistence. Gentle in his behavior, João applied himself to his studies, helped Joana with the housework, carried groceries home from the market. After dinner, we would sit on the porch and watch him play happily with the neighborhood children, giving them rides, and practicing somersaults.

Upon my return home one evening from the monthly meeting with parents, I found my wife quite disturbed: João had just vomited fire. I felt apprehensive also, realizing he had reached his majority.

The event itself, far from making him fearful, increased his popularity with the local girls and boys. He spent most of his time surrounded by lively crowds begging him to spit fire. The adulation of some, coupled with invitations and presents from others, slowly kindled his vanity. No party was successful without his attendance. Even the vicar considered his presence indispensable for animating the booths at the fair on our patron saint's day.

Three months before the great flood devastated the whole county, a traveling circus livened up our city, thrilling us with daring acrobats, merry clowns, trained lions, and a man who could swallow live coals. Toward the end of the juggler's act, several youths interrupted the show with rhythmic shouts and hand-clapping:

"We've got something better! We've got something better!"

Judging it to be some boyish prank, the ringmaster immediately accepted the challenge:

"Let's see something better, then!"

To the dismay of the circus personnel and the applause of the spectators, João made his way to the ring and performed his customary feat of vomiting fire.

By the following afternoon he had received several invitations to join the circus, but refused: it would have been difficult to surpass the prestige he already enjoyed in our own community. He even cherished the ambition of one day becoming mayor.

This, however, was not to happen. Instead, João's disappearance was confirmed, just days after the departure of the circus troop.

Fanciful accounts were given of his flight: that he fell passionately in love with one of the trapezists, who had been hired to seduce him; that he took up gambling and lapsed back into heavy drinking.

Whatever the reason, so many dragons have traveled along our highways since then. . . . Yet, no matter how vigorously I and my students—posted at the city gates—press them to stay with us, they refuse to answer. Huddled together in long lines, on their way to distant places, they seem indifferent to our cries.

Teleco, the Rabbit

*There be three things which
are too wonderful for me, yea,
four which I know not:
the way of an eagle in the air;
the way of a serpent upon a
rock; the way of a ship in the
midst of the sea; and the way
of a man with a maid.*
Proverbs, XXX:18–19

"Hey, got a cigarette?"

The voice was faint, almost a whisper. I stayed in the same position, watching the sea, while absorbed in ridiculous memories.

Annoyingly, the beggar insisted:

"Buddy, hey! Buddy! Got a cigarette?"

With eyes still fixed on the beach, I muttered:

"Listen, fellow, get lost or I'll call a policeman."

"Okay, mister. No need to get sore. But, say, would you mind getting out of my line of vision? I like to look at the ocean too, you know."

Exasperated with the insolence of whoever was addressing me in such a fashion, I spun around, ready to send him on his way with a good kick. I was stunned, however. There before me was an ash-gray rabbit, delicately querying me:

"If you don't give, it's because you haven't got, right, my friend?"

His polite way of expressing things touched me. I gave him a cigarette and moved to one side, so as to let him have

7

a better view of the sea. He didn't even take the time to thank me, because by then we were already chatting like old friends. Or, to be more accurate, the rabbit did the talking. He spoke of such extraordinary events, of such remarkable adventures, I concluded he was older than he seemed.

Toward the end of the afternoon, I inquired where he lived. He said he had no fixed abode, the street serving as his usual habitat. It was then that I noticed his eyes, gentle eyes, and sad. I felt such compassion, I invited him to come and stay with me. The house was huge, and anyway I lived alone—I added.

This did not convince him. He insisted I own up to my real intentions:

"It couldn't just be you happen to like rabbit meat?" He didn't wait for my reply. "If you do, better look elsewhere, because versatility is my one weakness."

And saying so, he changed himself into a giraffe.

"At night," he continued, "I could be a snake or a dove. It won't bother you, the company of one so unstable?"

I answered no, and we began to live together.

His name was Teleco.

As we got on more intimate terms, I discovered that the mania for metamorphosing into other creatures was, in his case, simply a desire to please people. He liked being gentle to children and the elderly, entertaining them with clever tricks or lending them a hand. The same horse that, in the morning, did so much galloping around with kids, come evening, gently walked the aged and infirm back to their homes.

He took a dislike to certain neighbors, among them a pawnbroker and his sisters, to whom he would appear in the skin of a lion or a tiger. He frightened them more to amuse us than out of malice. The victims, though, were not so understanding and complained to the police, who then wasted their time listening to persistent accusations. Even after ransacking our house from top to bottom, they could find no animal other than a rabbit. The detectives, therefore, grew irritated and threatened to lock up the complainers.

Only once did I fear that the antics of my restless companion were about to cause serious complications. I was receiving one of my usual visits from the police inspector when Teleco, prompted by a bit of thoughtless mischief, unexpectedly turned himself into a peccary. The change and the shift back into his previous form were too quick for the man to have time to scream. He'd barely opened his mouth in horror when once again he had in front of him merely a tame rabbit.

"Did you see what I saw?"

Putting on an innocent face, I told him I hadn't noticed anything out of the ordinary.

The man eyed me dubiously and, without saying goodbye, made his way out the front door.

Teleco played tricks on me as well. If I found the house empty, I knew he must be hidden away in some corner, disguised as a tiny animal, or even somewhere on my body in the form of a flea, busy dodging my fingers, running down my back. When sometimes I became impatient and told him to stop fooling around, it would, often as not, end in an awful scare. A billygoat would grow up under my legs and, like a shot, carry me out into the backyard. I'd be furious, and promise him a good thrashing. But, feigning remorse, Teleco would soon distract me with his affable chatter and quickly restore peace.

Then he would be once more that docile friend who charmed us with his unexpected magical tricks. He loved colors and often flew up, transformed into a bird of all conceivable colors, of an entirely unknown species or an already extinct variety.

"There's no such bird as that!"

"I know. But it's rather insipid to simulate only the known varieties."

The first serious clash I had with Teleco occurred about a year after we met. I was returning from my sister-in-law Emi's, with whom I had just had some serious differences over family matters. So I was in quite a bad humor, and the scene I stumbled upon as I opened the front door only served to fan my irritation. Holding hands, seated together on the living-room sofa, were a young woman and a shabby-looking kangaroo. His clothes were ill-fitted, his eyes half hidden behind a pair of ordinary wire-rimmed spectacles.

"What do you want, Miss, with that horrible animal?" I asked, annoyed at finding my house invaded by strangers.

"I'm Teleco," he interjected, with a slight laugh.

I stared disdainfully at the puny creature, with his sparse coat of hair, betraying such a level of obsequiousness and depravity. Nothing about him recalled the playful bunny.

So I refused to accept his assertion as the truth, especially since Teleco had no trouble with his vision and, if he should want to present himself all dressed up, would certainly have the good taste to choose different clothes, not these.

Faced with my incredulousness, he changed into a tree

toad, leaped on top of the furniture, hopped into my lap.
I flung him off me, filled with repugnance.

Recovering his form of a kangaroo once more, he questioned me with an extremely grave air:

"Is that proof enough?"

"Yes. And so? What do you want?"

"From today on, I shall just be a man."

"A man?" I repeated in astonishment. I couldn't ignore
the ridiculousness of the situation and burst out laughing.
"And that?" I pointed to the girl. "Is she a lizard, or a
young salamander?"

She looked at me angrily. She wanted to retort with
something too, but he cut her off:

"This is Tereza. She's come to live with us. Isn't she a
beauty?"

Right, a beauty. During the night I couldn't sleep, my
thoughts revolving around her, as well as on the idiocy of
Teleco's claiming to be a man.

I got up the next morning and headed for the living
room, expecting the facts of the day before to have dissolved into one of my companion's harmless charades.

I was mistaken. Stretched out on the living-room carpet
beside the girl was the same kangaroo, snoring loudly. I
woke him, pulling him by the arms:

"Let's go, Teleco, enough of this hanky-panky."

He opened his eyes, startled, but, recognizing me,
smiled:

"Teleco? My name's Barbosa, Antônio Barbosa. Right,
Tereza?"

She was just now waking up and concurred with a nod of
her head.

I exploded with rage:

"If it's Barbosa, out! And don't ever set foot in my house again, you filthy son of a rodent!"

Tears ran down his face, and, down on his knees in front of me, he clasped both my legs, begging me not to kick him out of the house, at least until he found a job.

Although I viewed with skepticism the possibility of a kangaroo finding work, his weeping dissuaded me from my previous decision, or, rather, to tell the whole truth, I was actually more persuaded by the imploring look that came from Tereza, who had followed our conversation apprehensively.

Barbosa had terrible habits. He repeatedly spat on the floor and rarely took baths, notwithstanding his enormous self-conceit, which drove him to spend hours at a time in front of the mirror. He also used my shaving gear and toothbrush. It didn't help very much either to buy these things for him, since he continued to use mine as well as his. And when I complained of this abusive behavior, he simply excused himself by feigning absentmindedness.

Furthermore, his ungainly figure absolutely repelled me. His skin was greasy, his limbs stubby, his heart secretive. He spared no effort to try to please me, reciting anecdotes devoid of humor, exaggerating his praises of my person.

On the other hand, I found it hard to tolerate his lies and, at meals, his eating, the noisy way he stuffed food into his mouth with both hands.

Perhaps because I succumbed to Tereza's charms, perhaps not to displease her, I suffered the uncomfortable presence of Barbosa without complaint.

If ever I claimed that Teleco's intention—to impose his

false human condition upon us—was nothing but non-sense, she would reply with disconcerting conviction:

"His name's Barbosa, and he is a man."

The kangaroo soon perceived my interest in his female companion and, mistaking my tolerance for possible weakness, he grew impertinent and made fun of me whenever I reproached him for wearing my clothes, smoking my cigarettes, or filching money out of my pockets.

On various occasions I appealed to his now slackening sensibilities, asking him to return to being a rabbit.

"Being a rabbit? I was never an animal. I don't know what you're talking about."

"I'm talking about a sweet gray bunny who had the habit of changing himself into other animals."

During this intermediate period, my love for Tereza wavered among dark fantasies which had little hope of ever being reciprocated. Still, in the midst of such uncertainty I decided to propose marriage.

Coldly and without hesitation, she closed the matter at once:

"Your offer is less generous than you suppose. He's worth much more."

The choice of words in her refusal convinced me she contemplated exploiting the talents of Teleco in a questionable manner.

Frustrated in my attempt to become engaged, I could not stand now to see them so intimate together, and I became aggressive.

The kangaroo noticed the change in my behavior and chose to avoid places where we might run into one another.

One evening, returning from work, my attention was alerted by the deafening sound of the victrola, turned on at full volume. Opening the front door, I immediately felt the blood rush to my head: Tereza and Barbosa, faces glued together, were dancing a lascivious samba.

Indignantly, I separated the two, grabbed the kangaroo by the neck, and, shaking him violently, led him over to the living-room mirror:

"Is that or is that not an animal?"

"No, I'm a man!" And he sobbed, his legs trembling, numb with fear at the fury he saw in my eyes.

Then he asked Tereza, who, on hearing his cries, had come to his assistance:

"Aren't I a man, dear? Talk to him."

"Yes, love, you are a man."

Absurd as it seemed to me, there was a kind of tragic certainty in their voices. I had already made up my mind, however. I threw Barbosa to the floor and started boxing him on the mouth. Then I drove them both out of the house.

From the street, though, she warned me angrily:

"I'll make an important person out of Barbosa, you swine!"

That was the last time I saw them. I did hear, much later, vague rumors about a magician named Barbosa who was having great successes in the city. But lacking further clarification of the matter, I concluded it to be a mere coincidence of names.

My passion for Tereza evaporated with the passage of time, and my interest in stamps returned. I spent whatever spare moments I had busying myself with my collection.

One evening, just as I was pasting in some rare stamps —I had received them the day before—suddenly a dog jumped through the window. When I recovered from the initial shock, I tried to shoo the animal out. I didn't manage to get rid of him, however.

"I'm Teleco, your old friend," he murmured, in a voice excessively tremulous and sad, and changed himself to an agouti.

"And Tereza?" I asked with pretended indifference.

"Tereza . . ." Without concluding the phrase, he took on the shape of a peacock.

"There were lots of colors . . . the circus . . . she was lovely . . . it was horrible . . .," he continued, vibrating his tail like a rattlesnake.

After a brief silence, he tried to speak again:

"The uniform . . . very white . . . five ropes . . . tomorrow I'll be a man. . . ." The words came out strained, disconnected, as Teleco metamorphosed into different animals.

He coughed for a moment. A nervous cough. Weak at first, he swelled up with his mutations into other larger animals, while I pleaded with him to calm down. Yet he was unable to control himself.

He tried vainly to explain. His sentences came out broken and confused.

"Enough of that now, try to speak more calmly," I insisted, losing patience with his continuous transformations.

"I can't!" he stammered, in the skin of a lizard.

Even after a few days the same turmoil persisted. Hiding in corners, trembling, Teleco kept whimpering, changing himself, on and on, into the most varied animals. He stuttered a great deal and couldn't feed himself, since his mouth, growing and diminishing according to the creature he embodied at the moment, did not always match the size of the food. Then out of his eyes poured the tears which, small in the eyes of a rat, bubbled enormous on the cheeks of a hippo.

Impotent to lessen his agony, I hugged him closely, crying. His body, though, grew in my arms, squeezing me up against the wall.

He didn't speak anymore—he mooed, cawed, brayed, squealed, howled, twittered.

Finally less disturbed, he began to limit his transformations to smaller animals, until he settled into the shape of a lamb, sadly bleating. I gathered him up in my arms and felt his body perspiring, burning with fever.

On the last night he merely quivered, until, little by little, he grew completely still. Exhausted by the lengthy vigil, I closed my eyes and slept. Awakening later, I perceived that a change had taken place in my arms. On my lap was a soiled little baby, without teeth, dead.

The Trap

*For if the trumpet give an uncertain
sound, who shall prepare himself to
the battle?*

I Corinthians, XIV:8

Alexandre Saldanha Ribeiro scorned the elevator and took
to the stairway, despite the voluminous suitcase he carried
and the number of floors—ten—to be climbed.

He was not in any great hurry, but his face clearly con-
veyed the certainty of an irrevocable intention. Once on the
tenth floor, he penetrated a long corridor, where dust and
debris lent a disagreeable aspect to the tiled flooring. All
the doors were shut, and no sound escaped to indicate any
human presence.

He paused outside the last office, long enough to read a
phrase written on the wall in pencil. Then he switched the
suitcase to his left hand, leaving the other one free to try
the doorknob, which took considerable effort—as if it had
not been used in a very long time. Even at that, he failed
to open the door, whose frame had obviously warped. So
he had to force it with his shoulder, and he accomplished
this with such violence that the whole door fell to the floor
with a great slam. The noise hardly disturbed him. He was
too sure of himself to lend it any significance, unconcerned
as to whether he should thus anticipate his entry into what

17

was a small, dark musty-smelling room. He glanced over walls and furniture, then cursed with disappointment. He had started to return to the corridor, with the intention of continuing his investigation, when he spotted a folding partition. He shoved it aside, only to discover a partly closed door. He pushed it open. He was about to set the suitcase down on the floor, when a sudden shock paralyzed him completely: seated behind a dusty table was a grayish-looking man with a serene countenance, who now pointed a revolver at him. Keeping the weapon aimed in the direction of the intruder, the man ordered him to stay where he was.

Yet Alexandre felt no urge to escape: nothing could have driven him from the present encounter. Any sensation of fear had been transitory, and immediately replaced by something more intense, as he gazed into the eyes of the old man before him—eyes of a painful shade of blue.

Within the room, everything manifested a state of decay, of complete negligence, down to the ragged clothing of its solitary inhabitant.

"I was waiting for you," he said in a calm voice.

Alexandre gave no indication of having heard, mesmerized as he was by the look of the man talking. It reminded him of the voyage he had made by sea, of some harsh words on the landing of a staircase.

The other insisted:

"You've come, finally."

Brusquely awakened from such reminiscing, Alexandre made a violent effort not to show surprise:

"So, you've been waiting for me, have you?" There was no chance for a response, because he continued, exultantly, as if some time-worn irritation had suddenly resurfaced:

"Impossible! There's no way for you to guess I'd be arriving today: I just got off the ship, and no one's been informed of my presence in the city! You're a fraud, a cheap fraud. Obviously, you've been up to your old tricks and had spies out on my trail. There's no other way to have found out, because I'm constantly traveling, changing my address and my identity."

"I know nothing of your travels or your disguises."

"Then how could you possibly guess the date of my arrival?"

"I guessed nothing. I simply waited for you to come. Two long years, here in this chair, the same position, anticipating your arrival, absolutely certain you would come."

For some time they remained silent, preparing to strike heavier blows or finally unmask the game they seemed to be playing with one another.

Alexandre considered moving to the attack, convinced that only thus could he wreck the complacency of his opponent. The latter, however, perceived his intention and anticipated him by insisting:

"Before you ask me any more questions—and I know you have quite a few ready for me—I'd like to know what happened with Ema."

"Nothing," he replied, trying to sound as unconcerned as possible.

"Nothing?"

Alexandre sensed the irony, and his eyes flashed with both hatred and humiliation. He tried to counter with a curse, but the tranquil intensity of the other's expression finally vanquished him.

"She left me," he allowed to escape, suffocating with shame. And in a vain attempt to display some remnant of pride, he added: "Don't tell me you knew about that!"

A slight glimmer lit up the old man's face:

"I guessed as much, but I wanted to make certain."

It started getting dark. The two were separated by a heavy silence as they both drifted back to reminiscing about matters which, even against their wills, would join them forever.

The old man set aside his revolver. His once ironic smile, which had lasted throughout their conversation, slowly disappeared. He lit a cigarette and meditated posing a question that later on he would find unnecessary.

Alexandre, however, prevented him. He approached the table, gesticulating wildly:

"Decrepit old fool, so you're not afraid I'll take the opportunity to kill you? I'd like to see your courage now, without the pistol!"

"No, besides your being unarmed, you never came here to kill me."

"What are you waiting for, then?" Alexander shouted. "Go on, shoot me!"

"I can't."

"You can't or you won't?"

"It's no longer possible. To avoid that temptation, long ago I fired every bullet into the ceiling."

Alexandre looked up and saw the ceiling full of bullet holes. He was suddenly confused. Little by little, recovering from his bewilderment, he succumbed to a fit of desperation. He ran to one of the windows and tried to jump through it, but couldn't. His head butted against a fine wire mesh, and he collapsed unconscious on the floor.

When he came to, he saw that the old man had just

locked the door and was about to shove the key out through the bottom.

Alexandre flung himself at the other in an attempt to prevent him, but acted too late. The old man had already surmised his intention and now enjoyed the panic which had overtaken his adversary:

"I expected you to try suicide and took the precaution of installing steel-mesh screens in the windows."

Alexandre's fury now reached a paroxysm:

"I'll break down the door. They'll never keep me here."

"No use. If you had bothered to take a look, you'd have noticed it too is made of steel. I switched the old one for it."

"I'll yell, I'll scream!"

"That won't help either. No one comes into the building anymore. I dismissed the employees when I evicted the tenants," and he concluded in a low voice, as if talking to himself:

"So here we'll remain: a year, ten years, a hundred, or a thousand."

The Bride from the Blue Cottage

*The fig tree putteth forth her green figs, and the
vines with the tender grape give a good smell.
Arise, my love, my fair one, and come away.*
The Song of Solomon, II:13

It was anger, not doubt, that led me to depart that same day
for Juparassu, where I should already have joined my future
bride, according to the note I'd just received from her.

Yes, it was anger. An uncontrollable anger that exploded
at the slightest movements of the other passengers, rude
enough to make those in the adjoining seats feel uncomfortable and wonder whether they were in the presence of
an idiot or a psychotic.

It was all Dalila's fault. Why did she have to write to tell
me that on the eve of her departure from Rio she had
danced several times with her ex-fiancé? If he had shown
up at the party by chance, and if it was simply a matter of
courtesy not to refuse him the dances, then why mention
the fact to me?

I don't consider myself jealous, but the letter irritated me
so that I found myself gritting my teeth every second in
order not to curse.

I calmed down a little after I realized from the sudden
changes in the landscape that within half an hour the trip
would be over and Juparassu would appear on the horizon

22

of the mountain, indicated by the little yellow station. I would only reach the cottages much later, after alighting from the train and traveling another two kilometers on horseback. And the first house would be his, the walls coated with whitewash, the oval windows . . .

I let the recollections envelop me and my imagination conjure up before my eyes the landscapes that represented the best part of my boyhood.

Without my noticing it, all the rancor I had nourished against my Dalila since the start of the journey was slowly evaporating. Not even my impatience to arrive got the best of me. I forgot all about jealousy and only longed for the moment when I would hold Dalila in my arms. I closed my eyes to experience more fully the desire to kiss her, to embrace her, and promised myself to say nothing of my suspicion or anger. I would simply tell her:

"I wanted to surprise you, to ask you to marry me."

The conductor on the train interrupted my reverie:

"You really want to get off at Juparassu?"

"Obviously. What's the matter with that?"

"Oh, it's just strange to see someone get off there."

Not knowing what to blame for the impertinence of the conductor, or his odd expression, I muttered a curse, which left him confused and abruptly begging my pardon for his natural curiosity.

Juparassu! It flashed into view, high in the sierra. Fifteen more minutes and I would be on the platform at the railroad station, awaiting some means of transportation to the house, where I would simply drop off my luggage and run to find Dalila.

Yes, to find Dalila. My Dalila, who, as a child, had freckles on her face and was always critical, argumentative. I could barely tolerate her, and our parents hated one another. Some problems about adjacent property lines and little incidents of animals breaking hedges only exacerbated the hatred between them.

Then last summer, on the occasion of my father's death, the neighbors from the Blue Cottage, along with the Americans from the two other houses, came to pay their last respects, and I was doubly surprised: Dalila had lost all her freckles, and her parents, contrary to what I had thought, turned out to be excellent people.

We visited one another, and one night I kissed Dalila.

Juparassu never seemed so lovely, nor its mountains so blue.

When I got off at the station, the porter very solicitously came to my assistance:

"You must be the engineer hired to make modifications in the line, right? Why didn't you let us know? We could have had a room all ready."

"Wrong, my friend. I'm no engineer and have no plans to work."

"Then what brought you here?"

Noting the sincerity of his astonishment, I refrained from responding uncivilly in the way that his question had seemed to merit:

"I intend to spend the vacation at my country cottage."

"I don't know how you could do that."

"Is it such an outlandish thing to spend the summer in Juparassu? What, is the place swarming with convicts and criminals?"

"There's none of that here, but it so happens that the cottages are in ruins."

I hesitated for a minute. Was I talking to a cretin, or had I been chosen to be the object of some disagreeable hoax? The porter, however, was quite serious and looked like a normal person. I decided, better not to insist:

"Where can I rent a horse, to take a ride in the neighborhood?"

His answer again disconcerted me: there were no horses in Juparassu.

"Why have horses when there's nothing of interest to be seen around these parts?"

I tried to reassure the man, since I suddenly realized he suspected me of madness. So I lied to him, saying I hadn't been back here for many years and my object was simply to revisit the place of my childhood.

The porter was relieved:

"For a minute you scared me. I thought I was talking to some crackpot." And very amiably he volunteered to accompany me on my walk. I refused the offer: I needed solitude in order to recover from the impact of such a bewildering set of events.

I hadn't walked for more than twenty minutes before I halted in astonishment: of my house there remained only the crumbling walls, half a fallen roof, with the forest invading everything.

Despite the fact that all this was evidenced to me with the utmost clarity, reflecting a reality impossible to deny, I still resisted. Circling the property, I met a farmer out back, tilling a small field of corn. I went up to him and asked how long he'd been living around here.

"Since I was a boy," he answered, lifting his head.

"Then you must have known this house before it collapsed. What happened to it? Was there an earthquake?" I persisted, in hopes of some redeeming word that would deliver me from this nightmare.

"Nothing like that ever happened. I know the whole story. My father told me."

Thereupon, he related that the decline of the region had originally occurred because of an epidemic of yellow fever, which was repeated again several years later, the reason for no one's ever returning to the place anymore. The owners of the cottages who actually survived were not interested in coming back themselves, but couldn't sell their properties. He added that the boy in that house was taken to Minas with his life hanging in the balance, and he himself had no idea if he actually managed to recover from the disease.

"And Dalila?" I asked anxiously.

He said he didn't know anyone by that name, and I had to explain that I was talking about the girl from the Blue Cottage.

"Ah! The bride of the boy from this house?"

"She wasn't my bride. Only my fiancée."

"No! You mean to say that . . . ?" He left the phrase unfinished: that you're the man, the boy who used to live here?

To avoid more questions, I preferred to deny it, repeating my previous question:

"And Dalila?"

"She died."

I was stunned to watch the tenuous hope I had nourished be shattered completely. Without saying goodbye, I headed back along the road. My unsteady steps could barely distinguish the rim of vegetation from the narrow forest trail as I climbed the little hill. From its summit I finally glimpsed the ruins of the Blue Cottage, glimpsed them without shock, without emotion. My capacity for emotion had ceased. My steps were firm once more, and from there within the ruins I would reclaim my loved one.

Faded and peaceful, the Blue Cottage stands before me. I walk through its wreckage. The stairway of tiles, partially destroyed. We kissed here. Kissed on the veranda filled with creepers, with rocking chairs, where for long hours we sat together. After the veranda, smashed full of holes, the hallway. Dalila would come to me eagerly. I climb the rotten steps of the wooden staircase. I reach her room: spider webs. Empty, my God, empty! I yell: Dalila, Dalila! Nothing. I rush to the other rooms. All empty. Only spider webs, and the windows buckling out of the walls, the floors rotting under.

I go back downstairs. I yell once more: Dalila, Dalila! Yell desperately: Dalila, my love! The silence, a brutal silence, answers my call. I return to her room: it seems that Dalila is there and yet I don't see her. Her diminutive figure, her gentle eyes and shining hair. She embraces me and I can't feel her arms.

The night peeks through the fallen roof. I still yell: Dalila, Dalila, my love! Sever this agony within me. I run madly.

The Edifice

In the day that thy walls are
to be built, in that day
shall the decree be far removed.
                    Micah, VII:11

More than one hundred years were necessary to complete the founda-
tions of the edifice which, according to the statement of incorporation,
was projected to have an indefinite number of stories. All calcula-
tions, blueprints, and technical specifications were quite perfect, de-
spite skepticism on the part of a certain professor in the School of
Engineering. Compelled to express his views on the subject—by stu-
dents who refused to accept the persistent reticence of their master—
he took malicious pleasure in ridiculing the project as "that curious
experiment of a different school of construction."

Once the last stanchion had been driven into place and the base-
ment was concreted, the Executive Committee of the Foundation,
which was in charge of the overall management of the project, pro-
ceeded to dismiss the remaining laborers and technicians, only to
recruit a new team of tradesmen and professionals.

1. THE MYTH

As for the purpose of such a building, nothing was con-
veyed to the engineer now in charge. Purposes, anyway,

hardly interested João Gaspar at the moment, proud as he felt to be directing—at the outset of his career—construction of the largest skyscraper that had ever been contemplated.

Attentively he listened to instructions from the members of the Committee, whose white beards, coming to a point as they did, invested them with an air of extreme pertinacity. They granted him ample authority, subject only to two or three stipulations which were to be scrupulously adhered to. His duties were not limited to those of a technical nature, but rather encompassed a whole order of complexities arising from such a unique enterprise. The smallest details of the project were to be entrusted to him, from salary adjustments to labor disputes. He was charged to eliminate even the potential for unrest within the labor force. This directive, they emphasized, had been issued to comply with an explicit mandate of the deceased founders, aimed at dispelling a current myth: that irremediable confusion would befall the workers upon completion of the 800th floor and result in the definitive collapse of the enterprise.

In the course of such painstaking elaboration by the Directors of the Foundation, the young engineer remained totally at ease, demonstrating absolute confidence in the successful outcome of the project. Still, there was a moment when he seemed slightly perturbed and muttered something ambiguous. The interview was already over—he was gathering up the papers spread across the table—and one of the elders offered this advice:

"In this effort, João Gaspar, there is no room for pretensions, so dismiss whatever notions you have of finishing the project. You'll be dead long before. We ourselves, who have assembled here, comprise the Third Executive Committee of the Corporation, but, like our predecessors, we have never entertained the possibility of being the last."

2. THE BRIEF ADMONISHMENT

The orientation he had received from his superiors he now passed along to subordinates, together with that admonishment which had so disconcerted him.

Aware that his audience was in fact more impressed with his speech than he himself had been with the old man's, the engineer felt decidedly pleased.

3. THE COMMISSION

João Gaspar was a meticulous person and detested improvisation. Before he permitted a single form to be poured with concrete, he instituted a Comptroller's Commission to supervise personnel expenditures, establish wage tables, and produce a Company Bulletin outlining daily work schedules. Such a measure not only resulted in improved productivity but diminished the potential for dissension within the rank and file.

To encourage still greater fellowship among those who toiled away at construction, a program of Sunday Social Activities was also inaugurated. As a result of this and other factors, everything seemed to be running smoothly, with work progressing on schedule. For every fifty stories so completed, João Gaspar held a special Company Dance, addressed his staff, grew old.

4. THE DANCE

The approach to the 800th story was marked by an uncomfortable foreboding. Precautions were redoubled and membership tripled on the Comptroller's Commission, whose activity was now incessant: ironing out difficulties, eliminating discrepancies, etc. Even the dance—normally held at the conclusion of each fifty floors—was deliberately postponed.

Finally, everyone's apprehension subsided. We had reached the 800th floor without incident. The event was commemorated with an even bigger party than previously.

During the early morning hours of the dance, however, excessive drinking, together with an incident of minor importance, suddenly provoked an outburst of incredible violence. Men and women lashed out at one another with absolute ferocity and transformed the salon into a heap of wreckage. As the chairs and bottles cut through the air, the engineer struggled desperately to assuage tempers, but never quite succeeded. A heavy object struck him in the head, abruptly terminating his conciliatory efforts. When he finally came to, his body aching and bloody from kicks and punches he had suffered while unconscious, João Gaspar felt positive he was the victim of a terrible plot. In an unexpected manner, the ancient prediction had come to pass.

5. THE MISUNDERSTANDING

Following this incident, the engineer locked himself in his house and, to avoid expressions of consolation, refused to meet with even his most trusted advisers.

Although it was clearly impossible to go on with his work, he at least wanted to discover where in fact he had miscalculated. João Gaspar believed he had faithfully adhered to the instructions of the Committee; if the result was a failure, the blame ought to be traceable to some violation of an unknown provision in the prophecy.

The insistence of his subordinates was eventually enough to overcome his obstinacy, and he finally agreed to receive them. They, in turn, wanted to find out why he had become so disheartened, why he no longer showed up at the construction site. Had he really been offended by the brawl?

"What purpose would be served by my continued presence? Hasn't my humiliation provided enough amusement?"

"What?" they protested. "But that was nothing but a drunken free-for-all." They seemed totally ashamed of what had occurred and begged his forgiveness.

"And is everyone still on the job?"

When the reply came in the affirmative, he heartily embraced his companions:

"From now on, not a single obstacle will interrupt our plans!" (His eyes were moist, but his lips betrayed a smile of triumph.)

6. THE MEMORANDUM

In an atmosphere of renewed calm, with all firmly committed to their tasks, another ninety-six floors were now added to the edifice. Things were moving along perfectly, and the mean productivity of the average employee was excellent. Propelled by a delirious sense of contentment, the engineer began to distribute bonuses, and dealt cordially with his staff, roamed the corridors and staircases, leaned out of windows, flitted here and there, and stroked his gradually whitening beard.

As if to prolong that initial feeling of triumph, slowly giving way to exhaustion, he decided to compose a detailed memorandum to the Directors of the Foundation. In it he planned to recount the special circumstances of his achievement and to refute the possibility of further prophecies that might interfere once more with construction. When the report was finally written, he took it to the office of the Committee, a place which he had seldom visited and, even then, only in the vague past. Instead of the compliments he expected to receive, a complete surprise awaited him: the last members of the Committee had died long ago, and—as if to exemplify, once again, the ancient myth's persistent power—the empty positions had never been filled.

Doubting what he had just learned, the engineer proceeded to query the Chief Archivist—the only surviving remnant of the once enormous staff of Company employees—as to whether some special recommendations for the continuation of the project had been left behind. But the Archivist knew nothing at all, not even why he still remained there, without patron or position.

Anxious to discover any document that might provide them with some sort of explanation, they abandoned themselves to the exhausting task of rummaging through cabinets and files. It was futile. They found only some technical specifications and a single phrase which surfaced repeatedly in the margins of books, memoranda, and blueprints: "Confusion will follow the 800th story and must be avoided."

7. DOUBTS

João Gaspar's euphoria now vanished. Gloomy and perplexed, he made his way back to the construction site. Atop the loftiest concrete slab, however, his thumbs tucked in his belt, he succumbed to a moment of petty self-aggrandizement, judging himself to be absolute master of the monument that lay beneath him! Who else could be in charge, now that the Committee was defunct?

His triumph proved illusory. Once home again, where the presence of any feminine touch was noticeably lacking, his doubts began to pursue him. Why should they have entrusted such an enormous project to an ordinary engineer? What could be the objective of creating so absurd a skyscraper in the first place?

The questions came and went, while the edifice grew taller, and the probability diminished of ever unraveling the truth of what had been born a mystery.

Slowly, his enthusiasm for work gave way to despondency. He complained to his friends of the tedium provoked by endless shipments of cement, gravel, and wooden templates, not to mention the anxiety he felt watching the ascent and descent of elevators.

At a point when his anguish seemed to be driving him toward collapse, he decided to gather the workers together for a meeting. Thereupon, he began to explain, with an emphatic wealth of detail, why the dissolution of the Committee now obliged him to halt construction on the building:

"We lack any further directives. Without them, I see no reason to continue working on an endless edifice."

His employees listened to him in respectful silence. Afterward a specialist in concrete, acting as their spokesman, responded resolutely and succinctly:

"Of course, we respect your authority as Chief Engineer, but our orders originate from a higher source and have yet to be rescinded."

8. DESPERATION

Futilely, João Gaspar pleaded with his staff to understand the situation. He presented strong arguments, but in a moderate tone of voice, since his aims were quite peaceful. And with equal politeness his employees refused to consider abandoning the project.

"Listen to me!" he begged, impatient with the growing obstinacy of his subordinates. "It can't be done, a monster with unlimited stories! The foundations would have to be reinforced as the number of floors was increased—that's totally impracticable!"

Although he always held their attention, he never convinced them. Finally, he took a more belligerent stance by dismissing the entire work force.

The workers simply ignored the notice of dismissal. Instead, they alleged the irrevocability of decisions handed down by the deceased Committee, and announced their intention to work nights and weekends as well, independent of further remuneration.

9. THE MISCALCULATION

Surprisingly, the staff's decision to work longer hours gave fresh hope to the engineer, who expected to see them vanquished by fatigue—no one could survive that pace for very long! He miscalculated, however. Besides their not showing any signs of stress, hundreds more began to arrive from the neighboring cities, offering to work without compensation on behalf of their comrades. They came singing, tools slung over their shoulders, as if prepared for a long and exhilarating campaign.

It was no use refusing to direct them. They selected jobs by themselves and worked enthusiastically, indifferent to João Gaspar's aggressive harangues.

10. PERIPATETICS

At first the employees would apologize embarrassedly for not always paying attention to what he said. With the passing of the years, however, they became accustomed to his peripatetic behavior and considered it a function of whatever instructions the Chief Engineer had received prior to the Committee's dissolution.

Not infrequently, struck by the beauty of his rhetorical images, some of the workers begged him to repeat himself. João Gaspar would get furious and burst into violent insults. Yet these, too, were so elegantly phrased that no one was ever insulted. Pleasantly laughing, we simply returned to the job, while the edifice continued to rise.

Elisa

I love them that love me;
and those that seek me early
shall find me.

          Proverbs, VIII:17

One afternoon—it was in the early days of April—she arrived at our home. She pushed open the gate quite naturally, which guarded our little front yard, as if she were simply obeying a time-worn habit. From up on the porch, where I was sitting, a needless observation slipped out:

"And what if we had a dog?"

"Dogs don't frighten me," she replied wearily.

With a certain difficulty (the suitcase she was carrying must have been quite heavy) she managed to climb the stairs. Before going in, at the front door she turned to me:

"Or men either."

Surprised by her capacity to divine my thoughts, I made haste to extricate myself from what seemed to be an increasingly embarrassing situation:

"Terrible weather out today. If it goes on like this . . ."

I cut short the series of absurdities that now occurred to me and tried, rather awkwardly, to avoid her look of reproach.

Then she smiled a little, while I nervously squeezed my hands.

Our strange visitor quickly adjusted to the ways of the house. She seldom went out, and never appeared at the window.

Perhaps at first I hadn't even noticed her beauty: so lovely, even when the spell was broken, with her half-smile. Tall, her skin so white, but such a pale white, almost transparent, and a gauntness that betrayed a profound degradation. Her eyes were brown, but I don't wish to talk of them. They never left me.

She soon began to fill out more, to gain some coloring and, in her expression, to display a joyful tranquillity.

She didn't tell us her name, where she came from, or what terrible events had so shaken her life. In the meantime, we respected her silence on such matters. To us, she was simply herself: someone who needed our care, our affection.

I was able to accept the long silences, the sudden questions. One night, without my expecting it, she asked me:

"Have you ever loved?"

When the answer was in the negative, she made obvious her disappointment. After a while she left the sitting room, without adding a word to what she had spoken. The next morning we discovered her room was empty.

Every afternoon, as dusk was about to fall, I would step out onto the porch, with the feeling that she might show up, any moment, at the corner. My sister Cordélia berated me:

"It's useless, she won't be back. If you were only less infatuated, you wouldn't be having such hopes."

A year after her flight—again it was April—she appeared at the front gate. Her face was sadder, with deep shadows under the eyes. In my own eyes, so overjoyed to see her, the tears welled up, and in an effort to provide her with a cordial reception I said:

"Careful, now we do have a little dog."

"But her master is still gentle, isn't he? Or has he turned fierce during my absence?"

I extended my hands, which she held for a long time. And then, no longer able to suppress my concern, I asked her:

"Where did you go? What have you done all this time?"

"I wandered around and did nothing. Except maybe love a little," she concluded, shaking her head sadly.

Her life among us returned to its former pace. But I felt uneasy. Cordélia observed me pityingly, implying I should no longer conceal my passion.

I lacked, however, the courage, and so put off my first declaration of love.

Several months later Elisa—yes, she finally told us her name—departed again.

And since I was left knowing her name, I suggested to my sister we should move to a different place. Cordélia, although extremely attached to our house, raised no objection and limited herself to asking:

"And Elisa? How will she be able to find us when she returns?"

I managed, with an effort, to conceal my anxiety, and repeated like an idiot:

"Yes, how will she?"

Barbara

The man that wandereth out of the way of understanding shall remain in the congregation of the shadows.

Proverbs, XXI:16

Barbara just liked to ask. So she asked, and put on weight.

Absurd as it might seem, she always found me ready to satisfy her caprices. In exchange for such constant dedication, I was normally repaid with scant affection and the renewal of obsessive requests. Impossible to remember now each one of them, so preoccupied was I at the time with observing the growth of her body, increasing its volume in proportion to the rise of her ambition. Had she allotted me even a portion of the attentions she bestowed upon things I gave her, or stopped putting on all that weight, it might not have bothered me so much to make the many sacrifices required in order to satisfy her morbid mania.

Almost the same age, inseparable companions throughout our childhood, we became sweethearts, engaged, and then, one day, married. Or, rather, now I confess we were no more than simple companions.

So long as the natural inconsequence of childhood prevailed, her eccentricities caused me no suffering. Barbara was a rather slight girl, and I saw no reason for her not to

41

acquire ampler proportions. With that kind of thinking, I took many a fall, climbing up trees to where the avid eyes of my companion had discovered tasteless fruits, nests of small birds. I also took a few beatings from boys I was obliged to provoke solely in order to realize a desire of Barbara's. And if I came back with my face all bruised, her satisfaction was only that much greater. She'd take my head in her hands and delight in caressing my swollen face, as if black-and-blue marks were some kind of present I'd given her.

Once in a while I would feel reluctant to acquiesce to her demands, seeing her become so uncontrollably fat. Still, my indecisiveness never lasted long. I was always over-whelmed by that look of hers, which would transform the most insignificant of requests into a formal demand. (Such tenderness lit her eyes, such a convincing air about her, when plying me with her extravagant entreaties!)

There was a time—there really was—when I pretended to be harsh, threatening to abandon her the moment I received one more request.

Up to a point, my warning produced the desired effect. Barbara took refuge in a kind of aggressive silence and refused to eat or converse with me. She scorned my pres-ence, hiding out in the backyard and infecting the atmo-sphere with a sadness that tormented me. Her body was wasting away, while suddenly her belly began to grow terri-fyingly large.

Thinking the absence of requests from my wife had somehow favored the advent of some new kind of phenom-enon, I panicked. The doctor, however, reassured me. That immense paunch merely presaged the coming of a child.

A naïve sort of hoping led me to believe the birth of a

child might eliminate once and for all Barbara's peculiar manias. And suspecting her gauntness and pallor were symptoms of some grave illness, I began to be afraid that the child, by falling sick as well, would die in the womb. To prevent that from happening, I begged her to ask me for something.

She asked for the ocean.

I didn't object, and set out on the same day to begin my long journey to the coast. However, once there beside the sea, I became terrified by its size. Scared that my wife might turn out to grow fatter in proportion to the magnitude of her demands, I took back with me only a small bottle filled with sea water.

At home again, I tried to excuse myself. She didn't pay the slightest attention. Impatiently, she pulled the bottle out of my hands and just kept staring, with amazement, at its liquid. She refused to put it aside. She slept with the little jar tucked safely in her arms and, when awake, would hold it up to the light, taste a little of its contents. Meanwhile she grew even fatter.

For the moment, I refused to concern myself with Barbara's excessive corpulence. My anxiety was focused on her belly, distended now in a horrifying way, to such a degree that, despite the dense mass of fat which covered her body, she remained hidden behind this colossal paunch. Expecting a giant to come out of her, I began imagining how terrible it would be to have to live with an incredibly fat woman and a monstrous child which might even inherit its mother's obsessive demand for things.

Much to my disappointment, an ugly, stunted little being was born, weighing a kilo.

From the first instant, Barbara rejected him completely,

not for his being so tiny and deformed, but merely for not having been requested in the first place.

This insensitivity in the mother, indifferent to the baby's hungry tears, obliged me to feed him in my lap. While he'd be crying for food, she simply refused to offer him her voluminous breasts, filled with milk.

After Barbara tired of the sea water, she asked me for a baobab tree growing in the lot next door to us. Early in the morning, once assured that our little boy was still fast asleep, I jumped over the dividing wall and into the neighbor's backyard to tear off a branch of the tree.

Back in the house, I refused to wait until daylight in order to hand my wife her present. I woke her up, calling her softly by name. She opened her eyes, smiling at having guessed the reason for my awakening her:

"Where is it?"

"Here." And I held out my hand, which had been behind my back until then.

"Idiot!" she shouted at me, spitting in my face. "I didn't ask for a branch!" And rolled over against the wall again, without even giving me time to explain that the baobab was much too fully grown, measuring almost ten meters in altitude.

A few days later, because the owner of the tract refused to sell the tree separately, I had to purchase the whole property for an exorbitant sum.

Once the deal was closed, I contracted the services of a number of laborers who, armed with pickaxes and a winch, uprooted the tree and lowered it to the ground.

Cheerfully frolicking, like a little schoolgirl, Barbara would spend her hours walking back and forth on the huge trunk. She also carved designs into it, inscribing names. I found mine, under a heart, and was deeply moved. This was the sole gesture of affection I had received from her. Indifferent to my gratitude for such a memento, she busily witnessed the wilting of its leaves and, on seeing the baobab all dried out, lost interest in it completely.

She was now terribly fat. I tried to distract her from her obsession by taking her out to the movies and soccer games. (The boy had to be carried around in my arms, because even years after his birth he remained the same size, not an inch of growth.) The first thought to occur to her, on these occasions, was to ask for the movie projector, or the soccer ball used by the players. She would force me to interrupt the showing or the match, with spectators protesting on all sides, in order to satisfy her whim.

I discovered too late the futility of all my efforts to modify Barbara's behavior. She couldn't understand my love and kept always getting fatter.

I had to let her act however she pleased and awaited with resignation her eventual requests. They were going to be the last. I'd already spent a fortune on her idiosyncrasies.

She approached me affectionately one evening and began to stroke my hair. Taken by surprise, I didn't immediately fathom the reason for such conduct. She, however, took it upon herself to explain:

"I'd be so happy if I just had a ship!"

"But we'll end up as paupers, dear. We'll have nothing left for food and our boy will die of hunger."

"The boy doesn't matter, we'd have a ship, the most beautiful thing in the world."

Irritated, I saw no humor in her words. How could she

possibly know anything about the loveliness of a boat if she had never seen one and only knew the ocean through a bottle?

I controlled my anger and once again set out for the coast. From all the ocean liners anchored in the harbor, I chose the biggest. I ordered it to be dismantled, and had it transported to our hometown.

I felt wretched on the way back. In the last car—on one of many trains that delivered the pieces of ship—my son was anxiously peering at me, trying to detect the reasons for such a vast and useless number of train whistles.

Barbara, advised by my telegram, was waiting on the platform in the station. She greeted us delightedly and even addressed some pleasantry to our son.

In the large, open space formed by the conjunction of several lots, Barbara supervised down to the last details the assembly of the ship, while I remained seated on the ground, bored and tired. Occasionally I looked at the child, who perhaps would never manage to walk on his little legs, and at the body of my wife, which several men, with hands joined, could not have encompassed, so fat had she grown.

With the ship now assembled, she moved her belongings on board and never touched land again. She spent all her nights and days on the quarterdeck, totally distracted from anything that did not pertain to the boat.

The little money that was left, after the purchase of the ship, quickly disappeared. Hunger followed, and the child would thrash his legs, rolling on the grass, filling his mouth with dirt. I was no longer very much moved by my son's crying. I had my eyes riveted on my wife, waiting for her to lose weight from lack of nourishment.

She didn't. On the contrary, she put on several more

kilos, and several more. Her exaggerated obesity prevented her from going down into the cabins, and her promenades were necessarily restricted to the upper decks, where she moved about with great difficulty.

I remained with the boy and, whenever I managed to escape my wife's watchfulness, began stealing pieces of wood or metal from the ocean liner, to trade them for food.

One night I saw Barbara staring fixedly into the sky. When I realized her gaze was directed at the moon, I set our little fellow down on the ground and climbed quickly to where she was. I tried with convincing arguments to distract her attention. Then, perceiving the futility of my words, I tried pulling her by the arms. It was no use. Her body was much too heavy for me.

Completely at a loss to know what to do next, I rested myself against the railing. Never before had I seen such a grave expression, such a set look on her face. This was going to be the last request. I waited for her to speak. No one else would restrain her.

But after a few minutes I sighed with relief. She didn't want the moon after all, just a tiny star, almost invisible, a little off to the side. I went to look for it.

Misty

*And every island fled away,
and the mountains were not
found.*

Apocalypse, XVI:20

It was not apprehensiveness, but hostility. It was enough to
see them go outside together and head toward the fields,
for my hatred to overwhelm me.

"You'll send him crazy, Misty!"

She would never answer, but just put her arm around my
brother as they ran off together.

At lunchtime Og always returned breathlessly, eager to
give me particulars about the new stars he had spotted on
his walk. At the least sign of doubt on my part, he would
simply appeal to Misty to serve as witness:

"Wasn't it a lovely star, Misty? So red! It looked like the
sun!"

"It *was* the sun, you idiot!" I would argue, irritated by the
morbidity of his imagination.

She always disagreed. With the meekest of gestures, expressing an attitude of understanding that sorely affected
my nerves, she would plead with me to believe him.

Such were the bitter arguments we had every morning,
after their exhausting strolls together in the fields surrounding the farm. Og would swear he had sighted blue,

green, red, and yellow stars, while I, absolutely convinced
that it was Misty who filled his head with that nonsense,
grew more and more exasperated:

"They don't exist."

Yet he insisted:

"You'll see them one of these days, Godô."

"Not Godô, jughead, Godofredo!"

Although he did show concern at being unable to convince me, he never seemed offended by my belligerent
attitude. With a vacant, far-off stare, as if he were addressing his words to the fields, or to animals out in the pasture,
he ranted on:

"They're so beautiful in the morning! The violence of
the colors, for a moment or so, comes as a shock. Later on,
the tones seem to soften, as your pupils adjust to the spectrum. . . ."

"Spectrum! What you need is a doctor to put an end to
this madness!"

Mostly, I would finish my argument with a punch in his
face, and Misty, calling me a coward, would take him into
the house.

I did not always regret my brusque behavior, but usually,
following such altercations, I would go find Mother and try
to convince her of the need for my brother to see a psychiatrist.

She continually evaded the subject, driven by some
strange affection she harbored for her younger son:

"Godofredo, you're in love with Dora." (Misty was just
a nickname for our foster sister.) "Why don't you try getting closer to her, instead of always punishing Og, who only
cares about his stars anyway?"

Listening to such talk, I simply became more irritated, without believing myself to be acting on the impulse of a possible grudge.

Actually, I felt no love for Misty. What did disturb me was her body. When I eventually came to realize, much later on, the true extent of my passion, I was already caught in my own contradictory feelings, and no generous sentiment whatsoever could bring me to confess a love that had grown sullen with rancor. Instead of trying to win Misty's heart, as Mother had suggested, I hit upon the idea of separating her and my brother. And the opportunity presented itself more quickly than I could ever have hoped for. It was when they had just come back from one of their long walks. I was out on the porch, reading the papers, unaware that Og had returned, since, contrary to his normal behavior, he had come in very quietly. Now he was pacing back and forth in front of me, until suddenly, unable to resist any further, he gave vent to the excitement of his latest discovery:

"This one has all colors, Godô. It's the most beautiful star I've ever seen. Look, just look!" And he dragged me out to the yard, pointing wildly into the sky. I refrained from my usual comments and ran to call Mother. No sooner had she answered than I brought her out onto the grass myself and told her to look at the sky: clear as never before. . . .

With a great deal of reluctance, she finally consented that Og be taken to see a doctor. While unable to deny her son's madness any longer, she nevertheless insisted:

"Only for a consultation! Not a word about hospitals."

Misty followed us, walking in silence. As we approached the entrance to the city, she finally spoke:

"You know he's not insane."

Actually, she probably wanted to tell me that I wasn't acting on any fraternal impulse. Yet, lacking the courage, or possibly realizing I would sense the true meaning of her words, she preferred subterfuge.

I avoided a direct response, which could have exposed my real sentiments, and proceeded to shift the topic of conversation:

"And what about you, Misty? Do you see his stars?"

"Not yet," she replied, lifting her head in the direction of the heavy clouds that now covered the firmament.

A few blocks before reaching the building where we were supposed to find the doctor, Og suddenly detained us:

"Look at that, Godô! You have to see it now, with all those colors!"

With such dilated pupils, his face absolutely transfigured, Og did seem to be the witness of some extraordinary spectacle which no one else would ever be privileged to contemplate. I was almost on the point of suggesting we turn back; yet I managed to control myself, but not the fit of tenderness which now overtook me. Trying to conceal the flow of my tears, I embraced him:

"Yes, it's beautiful, and don't lose sight of it, Og, because this is probably the last time you'll see it."

With his reddish, close-cropped beard and an unfriendly eye, Dr. Sacavém presented a rather grave appearance.

I told him about Og's mania, his visions, the reason for the consultation, but he hardly seemed impressed or even interested in the information I gave him. Instead, he limited himself to asking my brother to say something about his favorite stars. Og readily acceded to his request, enjoying the special treatment he was being accorded. So he repeated, with customary ardor, those stories he normally told us each day.

Bored with such a useless repetition, I interrupted:

"I don't believe in stars in the middle of the daytime!"

Misty, who had been quiet until then, began laughing:

"It's pigs you believe in, right?"

Although somewhat annoyed at seeing himself ignored by us, my brother still ventured to continue, his voice becoming more audible in proportion to his enthusiasm: enumerating constellations, relating their habits, colors, and shapes. And when he came to the polychromatic star, the psychiatrist demonstrated a rather perverse curiosity with respect to the subject, in an attitude I judged to be inappropriate for any professional. He seemed more like some amateur astronomer than a clinician.

In order to relieve myself of some of these doubts, I tested the reaction of Dr. Sacavém:

"Frankly, I don't really understand your methods."

"You will, later on, when we begin to treat your own case."

"My case! So you don't think only a crazy person sees multicolored stars?"

"No, I find nothing abnormal in that."

Then, more quietly, cleaning his glasses with his tie, he asked Misty if I always reacted in such a manner—irritated and hostile.

When the answer was in the affirmative, the psychiatrist came over and took me by the arms. He examined me intently and, frowning, shook his head.

I twisted myself out of his grasp and fled quickly from his office.

My mother was waiting for me there on the porch.

"They stayed, but I don't ever want to see them again," I shouted, running up the steps.

Sheltering only the two of us, the house seemed to grow larger. The quietness, too, seemed to increase within, where only my mother's eyes now formulated questions. Questions which remained unanswered and obliged me to escape into the fields, to wander along the roads. Yet I never went far. The recollection of Misty pained me. I had the impression that, any moment, she might step out in front of me, since she had always walked along those same roads, and now the hedges whispered the contours of her body.

My decision came to me slowly, in proportion to my longing and remorse. And until I reached the city, I had no idea what it was I wanted to do. Then, suddenly, everything became clear to me, and resolutely I headed for the office of Dr. Sacavém.

I felt, however, rather confused when I couldn't find the building I was looking for. At the location where it should have been standing, I found nothing but an empty lot. I stopped for a minute to orient myself, but it was no use at all. I couldn't come up with any alternative possibilities. It was that street. The only thing left to do was to make some inquiries, but none of the people I talked to knew anything whatsoever about the ten-story building I mentioned to them. The largest in the city, they assured me, had only two floors. And no one had heard of any doctor—among the five who practiced in the city—by the name of Sacavém. I combed the whole area once again, and made still additional inquiries: an anguished, futile attempt.

Eventually, I came back to that same empty lot, lay down in the grass, and gave vent to my desperation, realizing that I would never find Misty anywhere. I buried my face in my arms and cried to myself for a while. When I finally got up, as the afternoon drew to a close, a red star was glimmering in the distance. Gradually, it began to change color. . . . All colors . . .

Ñot Don José

Gather yourselves together, yea,
gather together, O nation not
desired.

Zephaniah, *II:1*

A violent explosion shook the city. Others followed: small and large.
Bewildered, people ran from one end of town to the other. One person
remaining calm in the midst of so much disorder shouted:
"It's not the end of the world!"
With the worst hypothesis now eliminated, other conjectures arose:
For an air attack there had to be planes.
"Artillery practice?"
Some concurred, "Probably so . . .," when pressed to explain the
mystery.
"And the artillery?" the more lucid therefore inquired.
There were those who even spoke of a mysterious invasion, until
suddenly everyone agreed: it must be D. José killing his wife with some
dynamite.
The populace hesitated to approach the building. After a short
silence, a couple of shots rang out. A drifter who refused to be taken
in by all the commotion remarked:
"Maybe the dynamite didn't do the trick, so he took out a re-
volver."
Faces turned pale. Anxiously, each awaited the outcome of the
drama.

1

Tragedy?

No. D. José was just setting off some fireworks.

No one wanted to confess the disappointment, indeed, the useless expenditure of imagination which, in that half-hour of terror, had loomed so large in the minds of all the spectators.

"He didn't get her this time, but she won't escape him twice. His hatred for D. Sofia is unbelievable."

2

D. José hate someone?

Outright slander! He loved his wife, the birds, the trees. She, yes, she was the one who loathed him and detested animals.

Conjugal adversity?

Hardly! The couple were admirably suited to one another.

But, among their neighbors, no one believed it for a moment:

"She pretends to love him. She's only after his money."

Idiots! D. José was absolutely the poorest man in town and suffered from a stomach ulcer.

3

The least hypothesis was countered with fresh arguments.

"And his children, weeping night after night, undernourished, spanked?"

Lies! Poor D. José had lost them all (there were five), victims of tuberculosis. Lately he recollected them by manipulating some kind of apparatus that imitated childish weeping and was much more upsetting than any children's tears.

4

D. José constantly spoke of a book he was writing. A book about goblins.

Did he write fables?

No. The goblins haunted his house, right in front of his nose.

Could his wife be one of them?

5

One day they found him hanging from a rafter. At once they said:

"He's just pretending. The knot isn't tight enough."

"Look at that sly face of his! He's mocking us all."

Infamy! D. José *did* commit suicide.

Why?

Everyone pretended not to know.

6

Years after his death, those who still defended him were asked:

"So, what did he actually do, this D. José, if he didn't smoke, didn't drink, didn't have a mistress?"

"He loved the people."

"And they?"

"They hounded him relentlessly."

7

Eventually, they erected a statue in his honor. It bore the inscription: DON JOSÉ SPANISH NOBLEMAN & TOWN BENE-FACTOR.

Final deception . . . D. José was nothing but a poor devil and possessed no titles of nobility: his name was simply *Danilo!* Danilo José Rodrigues.

House of the
Red Sunflower

Ye are the salt of the earth:
but if the salt have lost
his savor, wherewith shall it be
salted?

Matthew, v:13

The excitement was fevered, contagious. A physical joy
animated features which, until the previous night, had been
steeped in resentment. The events of before and after will
come later. What do they matter if for one morning our joy
was limitless!

Xixiu barely needed to look outside before he was hyp-
notized by the day. He seemed truly monstrous, bellowing
through the window at a universe which, besides himself
and my sister Belsie, consisted of four people:

"Nanico, you sneaking devil! Fornicating again, aren't
you, you slobbering gorilla!"

Nanico quickly dropped his hands from Belinha's breast
and answered sheepishly:

"Well, what if I am. . . ?"

Only Belinha, who was enjoying both the garden and her
partner's hands, felt annoyed with her brother Xixiu's in-
terference. Still, she managed to disguise her irritation.
Who could ever be irritated on such a day! With beguiling
naturalness, she turned to me, while I was busy kissing soft
Marialice over in a corner, and suggested:

59

"Let's switch, Surubi. You come here with me, and your dimwit of a brother can go to my little hypocrite sister for a while."

On any other day, such a proposal would have been rejected and have ended in an awful row. But on that hot morning, scorched by a blazing sun, the House of the Red Sunflower, with its immense gardens, far from the city and far from the world, was bathed in delirious exultation.

We had changed places without a word when Xixiu, dragging Belsie by the hand, came out of the house, spitting fire:

"My sisters aren't what you think they are, scum of the earth! Ah, if old Simeão were still alive!"

And he howled exuberantly:

"Disgraceful scum! You think mine are the same as yours?"

The sparks momentarily stunned me, but then I caught him with a blow in the face that carried all my two hundred pounds behind it.

He fell to the ground, laughing. Belsie, too, laughed scornfully. We all laughed: Belinha covered my lips with smiles and kisses.

Then her sister, averse to our crude exhibitions, suggested with insinuating tones that we go to the reservoir.

The first to agree was Xixiu, who didn't even bother to wait for a consensus. He hoisted his woman onto his back and galloped off down the road. We followed him, arm in arm, with Nanico trailing behind: accustomed to Belinha's sensuality, he was suddenly constrained by the ethereal air of Marialice.

We relaxed for a little while in the fields that skirted the dam. Not too long, since my companion, undressing, obliged me to do the same and dive into the lake. By the time the other couples decided to join us, Belinha was already tired of her devilishness underwater and, from ashore, beckoned me to come out of the water.

She made it difficult, though, since every time I tried to get a grip in the turf, she would step on my hands and force me back into the weir. I only managed to get out by swimming to the opposite bank. I climbed out and came running after her, furious, ready to give her a heavy beating. I grabbed her by the waist and squeezed her wet body with all my strength, until she screamed, called me an ox, and we tumbled onto the soft grass.

All of us were deaf to everything save ourselves, and then Xixiu, in a frenzy, threatened us with the past:

"Impudent cretins! If old Simeão were now alive, the shots would be ringing out!"

Belinha leaped up, stunned with terror, muttering the words of her brother between her clenched teeth: "If old Simeão were now alive . . ." She kept repeating them over and over, convulsively, insanely pressing her breasts against me. Her words took on an intonation of violent pleasure as, repeatedly, she glued her lips to mine:

"Old Simeão, monster. You're buried now, irrevocably lost in the noisome mouths of worms. They haven't any mouths, or lips, or anything, but still you are lost, tyrant, fiend!" (She brooded aloud, fiercely discharging against my body her satisfaction at the death of the old man.)

We all seemed to be tinged with some diabolical spell which now drove us to search anxiously, in pleasures, for the needed forgetfulness of those desperate days in the past.

Xixiu transcended even the realm of hallucination. On

his feet, like some resentful giant, he hurled forth his challenge:

"Old Simeão, damned Beelzebub! Let your body be manure fit for onions!"

He roared his curses, desecrating the memory of the dead man, and sank into the weir. He emerged farther on, revealing his stony physique, only to disappear once more, immediately afterward, around a curve in the lake. We hardly paid any attention. He'd be back soon enough, already mindless of the torments that, years upon end, we had suffered at the hands of our adoptive father.

Ah! If old Simeão were still alive! The filthy swine, the puritanical hypocrite!

While his wife, D. Belisária, was still living, things went well enough, with little longing on our part for the town in which we had endured with our families so much privation. A kind woman, she had delivered us from wretched hunger, to bring us up and console herself for her own lack of children.

Whenever our childish pranks got out of hand, Simeão, that powerful, primitive farmer, would look at us out of the corner of his eye, dissembling his sinister premeditations. His wife, however, refused to allow him to treat us like field hands, on whom he often used a horsewhip.

Years later, when the old woman died, her husband began persecuting us. His first measure was to separate us all. Xixiu couldn't even go near his sisters, nor Nanico and I near ours.

In order to communicate with one another, we had to meet together on the sly, after everyone else was asleep. Then one night Xixiu, the most rebellious among us and the only one to refuse to obey the prohibition, was caught speaking to Belsie up in the girls' dormitory. Old Simeão raised a dreadful outcry and, the following day, sent for a priest to marry them:

"I be a man of strict moral conscience and won't allow no goings-on in my house!"

Xixiu, just turned nineteen, wouldn't forgive him the phrase, or the rush to have them married. He and my sister had for some time nourished their own amorous vision, and the principal element in their fantasy was the wedding gown, with veil and garland, that Belsie would wear at the ceremony.

In order to goad my brother-in-law beyond the limits of his endurance, the old man refused to permit the newly-weds to sleep together, enforcing that same prohibition against our mixing with the girls.

From that day forward, they hurled insults at one another, on the slightest provocation. During one of these altercations, when Xixiu announced that D. Belisária had died a virgin only because her husband considered sex to be a sin, the two of them fell upon each other furiously.

It was a terrible fight. Although much less powerful than his adversary, Xixiu gave Simeão no opportunity to take advantage of his disproportionate strength. We admired, from a distance, the courage of our companion. Had the bout been with me, I would have quickly demolished the old man—no great feat, given my monstrous physique. I nevertheless reacted rather slowly and passed the time, as it amused me, contemplating the gentle eyes of Marialice.

They had traded punches for more than two hours when we began to suspect my brother-in-law was weakening, perhaps losing. Yet we did nothing to break up the fight.

Finally, at the moment when Xixiu took a heavy punch and suddenly fell, I went up to the old man and let loose with a dozen or so blows to his head. The last few weren't even needed. The first punch had been enough to stop him. The rest only served to stretch him out, unconscious, there on the ground.

The whole of our gang was deliriously happy. We helped Xixiu get back onto his feet and, together, danced around and around the body of our defeated enemy. Then we waited for him to revive again, but when he came to his senses, he didn't dare make a move, simply staring at us with rage. We continued our dancing indoors for the rest of the evening. (Any joyous event in our lives had to be commemorated with communal dancing.)

Retaliation from Simeão was not long in coming. The night of the same day, together with two of his workers, he crept noiselessly into my bedroom and dragged me, gagged, out into the yard.

They tied me to a tree and then horsewhipped me. Xixiu and Nanico discovered me the next morning, still tied up, my body covered with welts and clotted smears of blood. They cut me down, wordlessly, and took me into the house.

I spent days in bed, ruminating a profound hatred, contriving my plans for the total revenge I was to exact the moment I had recovered my strength. I would crush the old man underfoot, just wait! My brother tried to dissuade me. Simeão was now armed and guarded by a powerful mulatto.

My rage consumed me. I would spy on the slightest movements of my adoptive father all day long. . . . In the early mornings I always checked the door to his room, fronted by the Creole bodyguard. Ah, if I could only catch him sleeping, it would be the death of them both!

For three years this wordless warfare continued. Until suddenly one day the old man suffered a heart attack and died. Hardly had we received the news before we ran to find the girls, now freed of the old woman he had employed to keep watch on them.

And so we began our festivity. We tied up the old hag and then overpowered the mulatto. We dragged Simeão's bed into the garden, where we laid out his corpse, thrusting a red rose into his folded hands and spitting in his face.

The one who took the first beating was the old woman. The mulatto I ordered untied: I wanted him to myself, to crush him hand to hand.

When he saw he had only me to deal with, face to face, he rejoiced. Not for long, though. My punches, raining down upon his body, his face, with all the fury provoked in me by the recollection of his master, made him quickly realize he was lost.

After I had demolished him and he lay stretched out on the ground, we resumed our celebration of three years before. We danced and sang until the night left us exhausted. (Xixiu bellowed convulsively.)

That had been the previous night. Now our joy was limitless! We trampled upon the memory of old Simeão, desecrating the past! The day before, our spittle had soaked his dead face.

Hours had slipped away unnoticed, in the same way that our own delirium flickered out, which since the night before had set us afire. Nightfall was already dismantling the day.

Belinha, sensual Belinha of the white breasts, quietly covered her nakedness. Her eyes, bruised and distant, avoided my own unclothed body. We were preoccupied, and even more constrained in the presence of Nanico's and Marialice's euphoria: absorbed as they were in an ecstasy of mutual contemplation. My sister, apprehensive, disappeared and reappeared among the shrubbery that, farther out, skirted the reservoir. She was searching for our crazed champion. He was always playing such games with us: his ungovernable mind required a constant physical dissipation of energy.

An evil presentiment struck Belsie suddenly, and that moment she frightened us with a terrible cry:

"Oh, my Xixiu! Come back, foolish devil!"

She screamed again, driving us out of our momentary lethargy. We ran to find her and, shouting together now, hurriedly searched for him, again and again, along the banks of the dam.

Finally, we gave up hope. He would never return.

At night we walked and walked, all of us slowly realizing he had gone off to look for Simeão. We envied that glorious combat we would never see, his victorious cries as he slaughtered the old tyrant.

Belsie had to be dragged away. She wouldn't give up searching. Her face marked by intense suffering, her lips swollen, she wailed for her husband:

"Xixiu, come back. Xixiu . . . "

Her voice had lost its primitive ferocity, and prayers welled up in her throat.

We returned home exhausted, tormented. The absence of Xixiu, like a terrible weight, seemed to crush us. The desertion of our heroic companion marked the end of those glorious years of struggle against old Simeão. Xixiu would fight alone now, without our help, without our applause— but he would conquer.

Our silence only reflected our desire, fearfully repressed, to accompany his footsteps and witness the final combat. Yet none of us would dare take initiative.

He remained at the weir.

And we carried with us, from that day forward, his blinding memory. The House of the Red Sunflower crumbled beneath its own ruins. (Who would ever again spit fire and drive us into battle, decisively, with that bellowing cry of revolt?)

We understood that nothing was important now, nothing worthy of our violence or our passion. A contemptible future was in store for us. Belsie took shelter in her fierce silence. Marialice and Nanico—like two idiots—mooned endlessly at one another, far from any determination to have done with the world. Belinha, without her brother's cries, nevermore felt her flesh explode, and forever guarded to herself alone the fruit of her womb. And I, sheepish giant, was to live out my days with hands dragging at my sides.

A train whistled in the distance and, as it passed us by, let out a stream of sparks. From the coaches, which quickly fled, little silver pictures flashed into view: full of people. Besides us, then, there was someone else in the world.

We had to do something. So I walked resolutely out into

the roadway, stepping in front of my companions, and brought them to a halt.

Firmly, my fists clenched, I summoned them to the battle we must wage now against the shade of old Simeão. I outlined the plan of our campaign, I threatened, I roared. Yet slowly . . . my voice deadened.

They looked at me mutely, faces without hope. (Xixiu . . . He was dead.)

I gave up, defeated. It was no use trying to fight. Everything was shattered.

With humiliation, sensing everyone's disapproval, I turned tenderly to my Belinha and told her emotionally:

"This is the last day."

She didn't answer, but raised her eyes—lusterless, inexpressive—skyward and then lowered them to her belly. There the first petals had begun to emerge of a miniature red sunflower.

The Man in
the Gray Cap

*I, Nebuchadnezzar, was at rest
in mine house, and flourishing
in my palace.*

Daniel, IV:4.

It was the fault of the man in the gray cap.

Before he arrived, our street was the quietest in the city.
It had a wide promenade where the children would play.
Streets full of children. They would fill the wintry, misty
evening with sweet clamor, singing in a circle or running
back and forth from one tree to another.

Our uneasiness actually began the morning we were
awakened by the extraordinary commotion of trucks un-
loading heavy crates outside the old hotel building. We
were told, later on, it was all furniture belonging to a
wealthy bachelor who had decided to take up residence
there. I thought such an idea preposterous. Besides being
much too large for only one person, the whole house was
falling apart. The number of crates stacked up, all along the
spacious veranda of the building, suggested some less im-
probable hypothesis. Perhaps the place had been rented as
a warehouse for some commercial establishment.

My brother Artur, constantly at the mercy of an exaggerated set of sensibilities, energetically found fault with
my explanation. Nervously, he maintained that the houses

were beginning to shake, and he pointed skyward, where gray alternated with white. (Gray spaces, white spaces, perfect little squares in both colors, in quick succession, vibrant, pulsating.)

Well, this time it seemed my mania for contradiction had led me to commit a gross error in judgment, because before the week was out the new neighbor had arrived. Covering his head, he wore a (gray and white) checkered cap and, between his dark teeth, sported a curved pipe. His eyes were sunken, his baggy clothes overwhelming a tiny, almost skeletal frame that was being jerked along by a ridiculous-looking setter. Yet, instead of adopting the same derisive attitude I had assumed in the face of so grotesque a figure, Artur became completely upset:

"That man caused the checkered sky, but it won't be long before he disappears."

Very few would remain unimpressed with the old bachelor's behavior. His strange habits soon left residents on the street wholly perplexed. He was never seen to leave the house, but every day, at five o'clock in the afternoon, with absolute punctuality, he would step out onto the front porch. Never without his gray cap, which most likely concealed an advanced case of baldness, he simply took a few puffs on his pipe and went back inside. The rest of the time he seemed invisible.

Artur would spend the whole day spying on him, animated by a ridiculous desire to see him come out before the specified hour. Yet he wouldn't become discouraged each time his hopes were undeceived. His excitement mounted, however, as the moment approached to observe, once again, the solitary tenant of the neighboring mansion. And each time he spotted him, it seemed to make him absurdly happy:

"Look, Roderico, he's thinner than yesterday!"

I soon became annoyed with Artur and told him not to bother me, and that he shouldn't waste so much time on other people's lives.

He seemed not to understand, and the following day I would find him once more at his post, telling me again how the little man was dwindling away.

"Impossible," I argued, "that skinny devil hasn't anything left to lose!"

"Well, he's losing it."

I was still in bed when Artur came into my room, gesticulating wildly, and shouted:

"His name is Anatólio!"

I responded, quite irritated, barely holding back a curse: his name is Nabucodonosor!

Then, suddenly, Artur was silent. From over by the window, mute with excitement, he motioned me to come have a closer look. An automobile had just pulled up in front of the old hotel, and out stepped a lovely-looking girl. She proceeded to remove the baggage from the trunk by herself. And with a key, which she was carrying in her purse, she opened the door to the house, without anyone's coming out to greet her.

Positively driven by curiosity, my brother allowed me not a moment's rest now:

"Why hasn't she shown up before this? Isn't he a bachelor?"

"Look, what's so important about a young girl's living with an old bachelor?"

No matter how much I extended myself, trying to draw him out of his obsession, Artur would always manage to come up with additional reasons for being preoccupied. Now it was the girl who remained a secret, giving no evidence of her further residency in the house. Artur nevertheless rejected my idea that the girl had already departed, and refused even to discuss the problem with me:

"Strange, the man's wasting away and it's the girl who disappears!"

Three months later the door opened once again at the mansion, and out stepped the same young woman. Alone, just as she had arrived, and dragging her suitcases with her.

"Why on foot? Don't tell me the old devil wouldn't even give her money for a taxi!"

Following her departure, Artur seemed to regain his former interest in the emaciated figure of Anatólio, and, clenching his teeth, would mutter over and over:

"He keeps getting thinner."

On the other hand, my usual confidence in my own steadiness of nerves was gradually dwindling, giving way to a permanent state of anxiety. Not so much on account of the old man's chronic leanness, which mattered little to me, but because of my brother, whose afflictions began to furrow his brow and hollow out his cheeks. In order to prove to him that there was nothing abnormal about the old bachelor, I myself had begun spying on our enigmatic neighbor.

He always stepped out at the appointed hour. His eyes distracted, the hat swamping his head, he sometimes cracked a disdainful smile.

I couldn't take my eyes off him. His scrawniness mesmerized me. Nevertheless, it was finally Artur who called my attention to a curious detail:

"He's becoming transparent."

I was horrified. Directly through the body of the little man it was now possible to make out various articles there inside the house: vases of flowers, books, blurred by intestines and kidneys. His heart seemed to be hung from the handle on the front door, only one side of which was opened.

Artur himself was also growing thinner, but, even at that, I wasn't to be disturbed. Anatólio had become my only preoccupation. His flesh was rapidly fading, while my brother snorted with delight:

"Look! He's so thin now, there's nothing but an outline. He'll disappear tomorrow, completely."

At five in the afternoon on the following day, the old bachelor appeared out on the veranda, dragging himself about with difficulty. Having nothing left to lose, his skull had begun to diminish, and the cap, so baggy on his head, was sliding down over his eyes. The wind seemed to bend his body over. Suddenly, he had a spasm and emitted a jet of fire, which swept over the street. Artur, beside himself, savored every detail of it, while I, I backed away, frightened.

For an instant Anatólio experienced a violent contraction, only to vomit once again, directly afterward. It was less than the first time; then he tried to spit. In the end, anguishing so, he allowed some of his incandescent slobber to trickle back down his throat and ignited himself. All that remained was the head, covered by the cap. And his pipe, extinguished on the ground.

"Didn't I tell you!" Artur shouted, exultantly.

Yet his voice sounded wispy, remote. Looking at the spot where he stood, I discovered that his body had diminished to a horrifying degree. He was scarcely more than a few inches tall and, in an almost imperceptible whisper, was murmuring:

"Didn't I tell you, didn't I tell you . . . "

I took him in my fingers, before he should vanish completely. I managed to hold on to him a few more seconds, until he turned into a tiny black ball rolling around in my palm.

The Glass Flower

*But it shall be one day which shall be known
to the Lord, not day, nor night; but it shall
come to pass, that at evening time it shall be
light.*

Zechariah, XIV:7

What remained of the glass flower was only the bitter recollection. But still there was that longing for Marialice, whose every gesture was captured in the fields—at times green, but also gray. Her smile alighted from the rustic faces of settlers' wives, played on the polished arms of the furniture, lingered in snow-white walls of the villa. It accompanied the railway train that passed every evening as he watched from the plantation, and while the engine vented its sparks the whistle would shriek: Marialice, Marialice, Marialice. The final note was filled with anguish:

"Marialice!"

It was the old housekeeper shouting, and Eronides could hardly tell if the name had burst from Rosária's lips or his own thoughts.

"Yes, she's coming, she's coming!"

The unexpected reality shattered his composure. Nervously he slipped the black patch over a useless eye and proceeded to shave what remnants of hair still rimmed his scalp.

He raced downstairs, impelled by a bewildering sense of

happiness, hurried through the rows of eucalyptus until he reached the savanna.

Marialice stepped quickly down from the train to embrace him passionately:

"Oh, my Russian officer! How handsome you are!"

She did not seem to have aged the way he had. Her thirty years, cheerful and energetic, gave the impression of someone barely twenty-two—but without vanity, without having nurtured youthfulness.

On the way back to the house, he took her in his arms and kissed her lingeringly. She offered no resistance, so Eronides understood that Marialice had returned for good.

Hours later (the walls drank in the moisture of kisses) she began to ask about what he had done in her absence. He preferred to answer in his manner:

"I thought about you yesterday."

Night discovered them smiling, their bodies clasped together. He asked about Dagô, but she soon convinced him there was never anyone else, not before or after.

The flies of all the evenings, circling above his insomnia, had disappeared.

He woke up early, still clinging to the edge of a dream, looked beside him, and, not seeing Marialice, tried to reenter the interrupted sleep. Yet some new energy trembled within him. He flung himself out of bed and realized, in the mirror, his hair had grown back. His eyes sparkled and the black patch was gone.

He opened the door, and there was Marialice:

"Well, sleepyhead, forget about our walk?"

He looked at her in astonishment. She seemed so young and happy, her eighteen years lightening her slender body. He reached out to her insistently, trying to rekindle the previous night, silenced by the conviction that somehow twelve years had vanished.

The path was an old one, but something new seemed to alter its features. The morning began to glimmer, and the dewy grass was wet on their feet. He held his beloved in his arms and would interrupt their walk repeatedly with kisses on her hair. As they reached the edge of the jungle—the boundary to all their walks—a brilliant sun lit the sky. At the end of an open field he left her and entered the forest. Exasperated, she tried to follow him over the difficult terrain:

"You beast! Wait! Oh, what a brute you are!"

Laughing, without once turning around, scratching his face against the branches, Eronides disappeared beyond the trees. Now and then he could hear her cries:

"I hope a branch pokes your eyes out, you contemptible heel!"

From the jungle he brought her a blue flower.

Marialice was crying. Little by little, she calmed down, took the flower, and gave him a sudden kiss. Eronides stepped closer to embrace her, but she slipped away from him, running through the fields beyond.

Farther on, she tripped and fell. He held her there on the ground, while Marialice tried to resist, pulling his hair.

Still, they quickly made peace, for their love had been nourished by struggle and desperation.

Their walks continued at different hours and ending in the jungle. Occasionally, imagining he had finally caught sight of the glass flower on the branch of a tree, he would grasp Marialice in his arms, startling her. She would stare back at him silently, awaiting some explanation, but he always concealed the reason for such panic.

The end of vacation coincided with the final days of rain. Under a tremendous downpour Eronides took her to the station.

As the train began to pull out, the presence of the glass flower at once revealed itself. His eyes clouded, and a hoarse cry welled up in his throat.

The white handkerchief that waved from a window was the only reply. And parallel tracks, vanishing in the distance, condemned him to an irreparable solitude.

On the way back, a branch tore out his sight.

Three Names
for Godofredo

*The shady trees cover him
with their shadow; the willows
of the brook compass him about.*
Job, XL:22

Well, it just happened I spotted the glimmer of a wrinkle
in her brow. I can't recall exactly when she began to sit
across the table from me every day at lunch and dinner,
where for fifteen consecutive years I'd been the only cus-
tomer.

By the time I'd established the fact of her continued
presence, it already seemed perfectly natural to me. After
all, the spot hardly belonged to me, and, besides, my new
neighbor did nothing to provoke me. Let alone to address
me. . . . Her comportment during our meals together was
admirably discreet, without the slightest sound to call attention to her existence.

Yet, for some reason, that night I felt uncomfortable,
disturbed at not knowing the precise causes for her preoccupied look. I was already set to leave the table, convinced
that my companion would certainly feel more at ease. Perhaps she felt upset and wanted to be alone. . . . Looking
around the dining room, however, I couldn't help but note
the number of empty tables, which wasn't so unusual for a
restaurant whose clientele was quite restricted. I was struck

79

suddenly by the impertinence of my having to change my seat, when the girl could do the same. Besides, why had she chosen precisely to sit by me?

Still, I swallowed my irritation and, judging it in poor taste to entertain such thoughts in the first place, decided to get up and leave the table. After all, like myself, she just might prefer sitting where she was.

I turned to her and inquired if it would offend her to have me change my seat.

Her indifference to a gesture I thought to be as delicate as possible rather amazed me. I quickly excused myself with a nod, and made my way to the opposite end of the dining room.

No sooner was I sitting in a different chair than another surprise awaited me: the same young woman came walking over in my direction, with the obvious intention of rejoining me at my new table. At the same time, I was overjoyed —the frown on her face had disappeared—and I reproached myself for not having thought sooner to select a better table, or one more to the liking of my companion.

There was, nevertheless, something I still couldn't figure out: was she my guest for the evening? And what about the previous times?

Frustrated by doubts that now occurred to me, I asked her, a little self-consciously:

"I invited you out to dinner, right?"

"Obviously! And as if I needed a formal invitation to be here."

"What do you mean?"

"Good God, since when has it become necessary for a husband to invite his wife to their meals?"

"You're my wife?"

"Yes, the second. And I should also remind you that your first wife was a blonde, and that you murdered her in a fit of jealous rage."

"That's hardly necessary." (I was already sufficiently upset to learn of my marriage, and had no desire, therefore, to cultivate feelings of remorse over some crime with respect to which I hadn't the slightest recollection.) "I'd just like to have some idea as to how many years we've actually been married."

A bit theatrically, perhaps hoping to amuse herself at my expense, she answered:

"That's an old, old story. I can't even remember."

"And have we slept together?" I persisted, expecting at any moment to see the mystery resolve itself and verify, to my relief, its all having been just a matter of some well-contrived farce.

Her response, however, quickly undeceived me:

"Is that some joke? Of course we sleep together."

There wasn't much left to ask, but even so I went on:

"How about telling me when we first met one another?"

My persistence didn't seem to antagonize her, and I think she was partially amused at my growing sense of embarrassment:

"I only remember it wasn't springtime, the season for my geraniums."

I needed to know everything, despite a feeling of futility about prolonging my interrogations:

"My first wife didn't become jealous of our friendship?"

"Not at all. (And I wouldn't call it just friendship.) You, on the other hand, were the one who was always feeling resentful, and yet you realized—more than anyone—her fidelity. It must have been why you killed her."

"Don't speak to me of such a crime," I pleaded with her, reaching for her face, such a soft, young face. I studied her eyes, a gentle brown; she was lovely. Afraid of being rebuffed, cautiously I began to caress her tiny hands:

"I thought you might be a ghost."

"Nonsense, João de Deus! Why should I be a ghost?"

"It's just that, lately, I don't seem to talk to anyone, and I hardly pay attention to people. That's why it took me so long to acknowledge your presence."

I paused a minute. Looking around the dining room, I could see we were quite alone. In spite of my awareness that the restaurant closed early, I still resumed the discussion:

"My prolonged silence doesn't bore you?"

"Not at all, you've always talked to me."

I fixed my eyes on her once again: her loveliness was diabolical. Enough to vanquish even the desire to raise any further objections.

I waited until dinner was over before asking where we should go.

"Home, of course."

I confess I was curious to find out whether this *home* was to be different from mine. I couldn't really remember what it looked like and wondered if I could find it.

Even in front of the building which my companion assured me was ours, I hesitated:

"Are you sure it's this one, Geralda?"

She nodded, but I paid no attention. I was too busy, at that point, trying to figure out how I'd managed to guess her name, since I felt certain of never having pronounced it before that moment.

When the front door was opened, however, my doubts were assuaged at once: there was my overcoat with the fur collar, lying on the sofa. Only certain details still disturbed me a little, because I hadn't noticed them before. The furniture, although old, was quite sober-looking, yet the paintings, hung haphazardly around the room, were in strikingly bad taste. And everywhere there were flowers.

With perfect equanimity, Geralda quietly accompanied my successive discoveries.

I finally remembered my wife, once my curiosity had spent itself. Feeling awkward and uncertain as to how I should behave, I opened my arms to receive her. Pale-looking, with such black hair, such big eyes, she stood there in the middle of the room, waiting for me to come to embrace her. My emotions, the result of some inexplicable fear, momentarily held me back. I was finally helpless, however, to restrain my instincts toward that woman who now offered herself so completely. I hurried to her, seeking her mouth, kissing her greedily. I was savoring an entirely unknown pleasure, as if she were the first woman I'd ever kissed.

Only when I caught the glimmer of a yawn on her lips did I realize it was so late. So we proceeded to go to bed.

For an instant I found it strange Geralda should accompany me to the bedroom. Immediately, however, I realized I had no need to worry: there was a double bed, with two pillows. I also noticed the dressing table, cluttered with various articles of a feminine nature.

She began to undress, and rather embarrassedly I had to choose between quietly withdrawing or staying right there to put on my pajamas. Whether attributable to my own indecision or to the loveliness of her legs, I lacked the needed initiative and remained standing in the middle of the bedroom.

After she was comfortably settled under the covers, I sat

on the edge of the bed and started to remove my own clothes as well.

Then, lying there, sensing the heat of another's body, I was suddenly overcome by an incredible feeling of dominion, of absolute possession. I couldn't doubt it any longer —she had always belonged to me!

Softly, almost whispering, I talked on and on, as her hair brushed over my face.

The months swept by, and we avoided going out of the house. (I didn't want others to witness our intimacy, the attentions I lavished upon her.)

Garrulous, overjoyed, I loved to watch her eat now, carefully chewing each little mouthful. At times she would interrupt with some innocent observation:

"If the earth does spin on its axis, why don't we get dizzy?"

Far from becoming impatient, I would explain to her, in response, a great number of serious matters, which Geralda greeted with looks of astonishment. In the end, she extolled my intelligence to an excessive degree.

It wasn't long before the days began to linger, and my affections became routine, creating a void between us that left me quite taciturn. She grew equally reticent.

Only the restaurant remained, which we still frequented, but guarding the total silence to which we had so mournfully condemned ourselves.

Even her face began to annoy me, as well as the reflection of my own sense of boredom in her eyes. At the same time, the need for solitude again took hold of me; yet Geralda never seemed to let go, always pursuing me wherever I went. Timorously, I beseeched her with imploring looks, since I hadn't the courage to confess what was going on inside of me.

One evening I was staring at the walls for no apparent reason when, suddenly, I spotted a rope hanging from a nail. I took it down and remarked to Geralda, who seemed very aloof, detached:

"It would make a nice necklace."

She didn't deny it, and offered her neck, around which I looped the rope. Then I pulled both ends. My wife closed her eyes as if she were receiving a caress. I squeezed tighter and watched her slump to the floor.

Since it was already time for dinner, I headed for the restaurant, automatically, where I took the usual table. I sat there distractedly, with no feeling of apprehensiveness. On the contrary, I was totally absorbed in a sense of my own liberation. I hadn't yet chosen from the menu when I felt a slight shiver: in the chair opposite mine, a young woman sat down who, had it not been for the blond hair, I would have sworn was my wife. The likeness was uncanny. The same lips, nose, eyes, and that way of wrinkling the brow.

After regaining my composure, I tried to get to the bottom of the mystery:

"Is it you, Geralda?" (The question was more for the purpose of initiating a conversation than to obtain an affirmative answer. My wife had black hair and a gold tooth.)

"No, I'm the first wife; you just murdered the second."

"Yes, I already know that . . . in a fit of jealous rage."

"And could it be any different, my poor Robério?"

"Robério?" (No one had ever known me by that name.

There had to be some mistake, some terrible deception behind all of this.)

I struggled to control myself sufficiently in order to clear up the misunderstanding:

"It's all over with, Joana. My name is Godofredo."

"You're mistaken, Robério. You can't forget."

"And why not?" I shouted aggressively, losing my patience at her self-assurance.

She dismissed my anger. Indifferent, irritatingly calm, she continued to provoke me:

"Yell as much as you want; the restaurant's empty."

"And why is it so empty?" I demanded harshly, raising my voice to an even higher pitch of anger.

Joana recognized the futility of an explanation, but answered me just the same, attempting only to conceal her pity:

"Because just the two of us come to this restaurant. Father bought it for you."

"I never asked anything from your father, and had no idea he even existed. To hell with the both of you!"

In the midst of nausea and terror, I hurriedly got up from the table. I quickly made it to the door and ran down the street, with no idea of what to do next.

I only stopped when I reached the iron gate in front of the house. I bolted it behind me and, once inside the house, locked the front door as well. I'd barely put the keys in my pocket when I remembered Geralda's corpse. Just as it occurred to me to leave, I checked myself: before me, standing there in the vestibule, was a woman who looked completely similar to my other wives. She had Joana's blond hair, but was distinguished from both by having, aside from the pair of arched eyebrows, an amethyst ring on her wedding finger.

I was overwhelmed by a desperate feeling. I reached out to her, and she quickly snuggled into my arms, glueing her body tightly to mine. I lifted my hands to her neck and squeezed.

She lay stretched out on the carpet, and I headed for the kitchen. As I entered the dining room, I halted: at the head of the table, ready for the evening meal, smiled another young girl, again of extraordinary likeness to Joana and Geralda.

"Naturally, you must be the fourth wife?"

"No, João de Deus, we're simply engaged to be married," she said, offering me a seat at her left.

"My fiancée?" Bewildered, I inquired if we'd been living together very long.

"I've lived by myself since my parents passed away. Now that you're here, you'll be my guest. And after we get married, we can move to your city."

The velvet ribbon fastening the antique medallion around Isabel's neck suddenly fascinated me. I averted my gaze by looking down at my plate, already served, and I slowly realized my appetite was gone. When I looked up again, it occurred to me to formulate some questions, possibly the same ones I'd asked my second wife that first night at the restaurant. I gave up, though, preoccupied now with the problem of rediscovering that city which had been lost in my memory.

Alfredo

This is the generation of them
that seek him, that seek thy face,
O God of Jacob.

Psalms, *xxiv:6*

Weary I came, weary I return.

Our first conjugal dispute arose when the beast threatened to attack the valley. Joaquina, like most of the villagers, was worried about the peculiar sounds echoing down the mountainside.

Initially, she tried to get me to share her silly superstitions. I laughed at her credulousness: imagine, a werewolf! That's all that was needed!

When I discovered she wasn't kidding, but was actually touchy about my sarcasms, I attempted to make her realize that the supernatural doesn't exist. She refused to take my arguments seriously: we were at odds, and both of us held very definite points of view.

As the days went by, the animal's cries grew more shrill, and my wife cursed me, indignant before my continuing skepticism.

Quietly, I began to consider the phenomenon: hoping to unmask the origin of such sounds. The message they carried was so painfully oppressive, of flesh transpierced with needles.

For a while I still hoped the beast would abandon his

hiding place and come down to confront us. Since he delayed, however, I made up my mind to go look for him, despite the protests of my wife, who threatened to leave me for good if I should persist with my intention.

I set out on my journey at dawn. By evening, after an exhausting trek, I had found the animal.

I wasn't afraid to face him. On the contrary, I felt rather moved, sensing all the tenderness that emanated from such childlike eyes.

Without any sign of aggression, from time to time he lifted his head—tiny—ridiculous, in fact—and howled. His disfigured dromedary shape was almost funny.

A feeble smile flickered within me, but failed to touch my lips, contorted with pity.

Carefully, so as not to frighten him, I stepped closer. Now only a small distance separated the two of us, as, timidly, I asked him what he wanted from us and to whom he was directing so lugubrious a message. He wouldn't answer.

I refused to accept his silence and insisted more vehemently:

"Where do you come from? Why won't you go down to the village? I expected you for so long!"

My self-consciousness only increased as I repeated my questions, to no avail. Eventually, realizing that talk was futile, I lost all patience:

"And what are you doing here, planted on this mountaintop like an idiot?"

He stopped his howling and stared at me with undisguised curiosity. Then, without taking off his hat, he muttered:

"Drinking water."

The phrase, pronounced with a certain difficulty, in a tired voice, full of tedium, revealed the meaning of his message to me.

There in front of me was my brother Alfredo, who had stayed behind when I set out to find somewhere the tranquillity the plateau had never afforded me.

Nor was I ever to find it in the valley. That's why he'd come to look for me.

After kissing his bristly face and hugging his skinny neck, I tied a rope around him. We began our descent with careful steps, heading for the village below.

When we crossed the main street, no one appeared at the windows, as if the arrival of my brother were the most banal of happenings. I concealed my fury and pulled him along the narrow, badly paved street that led to my house.

Joaquina was there at the door. Without exchanging a word of greeting, I pushed her out of the way with an arm. She moved right back to the same spot, gave me a shove herself, and announced she wouldn't consent to keep such an animal in the house.

"You're the animal! This is my brother Alfredo. I won't allow you to insult him that way."

"Since you won't allow it, then out with the both of you!"

Alfredo, who was watching our squabble with total detachment, now ventured to interrupt the discussion with an ill-advised observation:

"Very interesting . . . The lady has two different eyes: one green and the other blue."

Vexed by his comment, Joaquina gave him a slap in the face, and he lowered his head in humiliation.

I felt an irresistible urge to beat my wife, but my brother

began to walk, sluggishly, pulling me along by the rope I was holding.

By nightfall we found ourselves high in the sierra once more. Down below, tiny lights still indicated the existence of a village. Hunger and fatigue oppressed me: furthermore, I couldn't seem to prevent my past from now unfolding painfully before me. It came back jaggedly, brutal.

("Joaquim Boaventura, son of a bitch!" His enormous fat hands reached out for my throat. I dropped the stolen piece from my hand and, trembling, awaited my punishment.)

Son of a bitch, all right. Such illusions, my flight from the plateau, imagining I might find some happiness at the other side of the mountains. Son of a bitch!

Alfredo asked if we couldn't rest a little. He folded his legs underneath himself and let me pat his head.

He too had wandered far and senselessly. In his case, however, he had fled much too far in trying to isolate himself, to escape from mankind; whereas I had merely looked to the valley for an impossible serenity.

Initially, Alfredo had thought a solution would be to turn into a pig, convinced as he was of the impossibility of living among his own kind, who seemed to devour one another with hatred. He tried to appease them, only to have them turn upon him.

Transformed into a pig, he lost any vestige of tranquillity. Instead, he spent every minute digging in the muddy ground. And he had to fight constantly with his companions, without an apparent reason for such behavior.

Then he thought that dissolving into a cloud might somehow decide things. Decide what? Well, he had to decide something. It was at that very instant it occurred to him to change into the verb *decide*.

And the pig became verb. A tiny verb: unconjugatible.

Nevertheless, the verb *decide* is, obviously, the solution to problems, the remedy for ills. He had no rest in that condition either, compelled to decide matters, yet failing to provide a solution to so many of them. When they asked him to step into one more family quarrel, he refused:

"No more of this!"

And he turned into a dromedary, hoping that to drink water the rest of his life would be a less demanding occupation.

Morning found us still high in the mountains. I took a last look at the village down below, hazed by the misty drizzle falling. I had wasted a day searching the mountains for a refuge against the nausea of the past. Once again I was to wander through strange lands, crossing still other cordilleras, blue like all of them. I would come to valleys and plains, hearing rocks thunder, feeling the cold, sunless mornings. And this time with no hope of a stopping place.

Alfredo, softened by the look of melancholy which stained my eyes, began licking my face with his rough tongue. Getting up, I pulled him by the rope as we started our slow descent down the mountain.

Yes, weary I came and weary I return.

The Moon

Lo, let that night be
solitary, let no joyful
voice come therein.
Job, III:7

No light, no moon. The sky and streets were dark, compromising, in a way, to my plans. Yet my patience was truly inexhaustible, and I had only to shadow Cris's footsteps. So every night, after dinner, I stood outside his dwelling, leaning against the wall and waiting. I took no precautions to hide myself or otherwise prevent him from seeing me, since he never troubled himself about what might be going on around him. The total darkness which engulfed us and the swiftness with which he made it to the sidewalk when leaving his house never allowed me to catch a glimpse of his actual physiognomy. He always proceeded resolutely down the street, as if with some fixed destination in mind. Little by little, though, his movements would become slower, more indecisive, and belie the earlier determinedness. I followed him with difficulty. Vile and menacing shadows stretched over me and forced me back into unavoidable detours. The unseen hovered all about me, yet Cris made his way effortlessly, unimpeded and undisturbed. If it weren't for his repeatedly stopping, the job would have turned out to be impossible. And whenever I finally caught

93

up with him, after having lost him for several minutes, he would be crouching over and filling his inner pockets with articles almost impossible to distinguish at such distance.

It was horribly monotonous, pursuing him always along the same streets. Especially since he never went into any building, or conversed with women or friends, or even said so much as hello to an acquaintance.

Upon returning, early in the morning, Cris would take from inside his jacket all the objects he had collected on his walk and, one at a time, toss them away. I had the impression that he contemplated them with a certain tenderness before letting them go.

Even after a few months had elapsed, his walks still followed the same fixed pattern. Yes, the circuitous path of Cris was invariable: starting from his house, he would go ten blocks down, turning on the second boulevard along his route. From there he would continue for a short distance, cutting off immediately onto a narrow, twisting street. Within fifteen minutes or so, he arrived at the outskirts of the city, where buildings were few and poorly kept. Invariably, he halted only when reaching a certain haberdasher's shop, in whose window, dressed with crepe paper, was to be found, on permanent display, a pitiful-looking dolly. It had blue eyes and a plaster smile.

One night—I was now accustomed to the dead of night —I discovered with mild surprise that his steps didn't lead us along the previous day's itinerary. (There was something that hadn't sufficiently matured, yet, to deal with so sudden a break.)

On that day, then, with a firm step, he kept going straight

ahead, skipping the cross streets, which he passed without stopping. Instead, he cut directly across the center of town, avoiding the boulevard along which the wholesale trade was located. He paused only once—and then just briefly—in front of a cinema in which children from other times used to watch film serials. He made a gesture, almost as if to buy a ticket, which certainly alarmed me. However, his indecision was simply momentary, and he proceeded on his walk. He threaded his way down the streets of prostitution, stopping, at intervals, before doorways, peeking in windows, almost all of them at ground level.

In front of a low house, the only one in the city that appeared to be lit, he paused hesitantly. I had an intuition it would be at that precise instant, since if Cris started back, I would be left with no other opportunity. So I ran up beside him and drew out my dagger, sinking it into his back. Without a cry, only the slightest death rattle, he slumped to the ground. From his thin corpse the moon emerged. A passing prostitute, perhaps moved by some thoughtless gesture, grabbed it in her hands, while a silver drizzle covered the clothes of the deceased. The woman, noticing what she held in her fingers, broke into convulsive weeping. Abandoning the moon, which floated into space, she buried her head against my shoulder. I pushed her aside and knelt down to contemplate Cris's face. It was a childish face with a plaster smile and blue eyes.

Zacarias, the Pyrotechnist

And thine age shall be clearer than the noonday; thou shalt shine forth, thou shalt be as the morning star.

Job, XI:17

Rare is the occasion when, in conversations among friends of mine or people of my acquaintance, this question doesn't arise: was the pyrotechnist Zacarias actually dead?

Opinions differ in this respect. Some think I am alive—the dead man merely bore some resemblance to me. Others, more superstitious, believe that my death pertains to the roster of accomplished facts, and that the individual whom they persist in calling Zacarias is nothing but a tormented soul wrapped in some pitiable human garb. There are still others who assert, categorically, the fact of my death, and so refuse to acknowledge the existent citizen to be Zacarias—specialist in fireworks—but rather someone quite similar to the deceased.

One thing no one discusses: that if Zacarias did in fact die, his body was not interred.

The only person qualified to provide accurate information on the subject is myself. However, I am prevented from doing so because my friends run away from me as soon as they catch a glimpse of me from a distance. If taken by surprise, they stand there appalled, unable to utter even a word.

In point of fact I did die, which corroborates the version espoused by those believing in my death. On the other hand, I am also not dead, since I do everything that I did previously and, I have to say, with greater alacrity than ever before.

First it was blue, then green, yellow, and black. A heavy black, full of red stripes, of a deep red, resembling dense ribbons of blood. Pasty blood with yellowish pigments, of a greenish yellow, pale, almost without color.

When everything began to go white, a car came by and killed me.

"Simplício Santana de Alvarenga!"

"Present!"

I felt my head spin, my body roll, as if I were lacking any support from the ground beneath me. I was immediately dragged along by an irresistibly powerful force. I tried to grab onto trees, whose twisted branches, pulled upward, slipped from my fingers. Farther along, I reached out with both hands for a wheel of fire, which began to whirl between them at tremendous speed, without, however, burning them.

"Friends: in the midst of struggles only the fittest survive, and the moment of supreme sacrifice is at hand. Those who would wish to act in time, take off your hats!"

(Beside me danced fireworks, immediately swallowed up by the rainbow.)

"Simplício Santana de Alvarenga!"

"Not here?"

"Take your hand out of your mouth, Zacarias!"

"How many continents are there?"

"And Oceania?"

Children's playthings were to come no longer from the seas of China.

The schoolmistress, bony, skinny, her eyes glazed-looking, was holding a dozen skyrockets in her right hand. The rods were quite long, long enough to oblige D. Josefina to place her feet apart some two meters above the floor, while her head, covered with strands of twine, almost bumped against the ceiling.

"Simplício Santana de Alvarenga!"

"Children, respect the truth!"

The night was dark. No, black. It didn't take long for white filaments to cover the sky.

I was walking along the road. Acaba-Mundo Road: a few curves, silence, more shadows than silence.

The car did not honk from the distance. And even when it was practically on top of me, I somehow failed to notice the headlights, most likely because it wasn't the right night for whiteness to touch the earth.

The girls in the car shrieked hysterically and proceeded to faint. The fellows talked together in low voices, instantly cured of their drunkenness, and began discussing what might be the best way to deal with the corpse.

First it was blue, then green, yellow, and black. A heavy black, full of red stripes, of a deep red, resembling dense ribbons of blood. Pasty blood with yellowish pigments, of a greenish yellow, almost without color. I'd never want to live without color. To live, to get muscles good and tired, walking along streets filled with people, empty of men.

There was silence, more shadows than silence, because the fellows were no longer discussing the matter quietly. They now spoke in natural tones, suitably laced with slang.

The atmosphere, likewise, was relaxed and calm, and the cadaver—my bloodstained corpse—in no way objected to the end these fellows wanted to bestow on it.

The initial idea, rejected almost at once, was to drive me into the city, where they might dispose of me, conveniently, at the morgue. After a brief debate, during which every argument was coldly scrutinized, the opinion prevailed that my body might dirty the car. And there was still an additional bother: the probable unwillingness of the girls to ride together with a corpse. (On this point they were roundly mistaken, as I will explain further on.)

One of the fellows, a strapping beardless youth—the only one to have been deeply disturbed by the accident, who remained silently distressed throughout the course of these events—suggested they should leave the girls on the road there and proceed to carry me to the cemetery. His friends, though, paid no attention to his proposal. They limited themselves to sneering at Jorge's bad taste—as they called it—and at the ridiculousness of being more concerned with the fate of a cadaver than with the lovely little ladies who were still in the car.

The boy thereupon acknowledged the stupidity of what he had just said and, without looking directly at the other members of the circle, began to whistle, obviously quite embarrassed.

Impossible not to feel an immediate sympathy for him, in the light of his reasonable suggestion, expressed rather poorly to those who were busy deciding my fate. Anyway, long walks tire indiscriminately the living and the dead. (This argument did not occur to me at the time.)

They went on to consider other possible solutions and, finally, decided that throwing me into a ditch—a deep ditch which skirted the roadway—then cleaning up the bloodstained pavement and meticulously washing the car when back home, was the solution most adequate to the case, and one that best suited any possible complications with the police, ever eager to find mystery where none abided.

But that had to be one of the few suggestions that did not interest me. The idea of lying around dumped into a hole, among the stones and weeds, was unendurable to me. And, besides, my body might, after being rolled into the gully, remain hidden among all the vegetation, soil, and gravel. If that should happen, it would never be discovered in its improvised tomb, and my name would likewise fail to make the headlines in any of the daily papers.

No, I was not to be robbed of that, even if only of a small obituary in the principal morning newspaper. I had to act quickly, decisively:

"That's enough! It's my turn to be heard."

Jorge paled, let out a dull moan, and passed out, while his friends, though astonished at seeing a cadaver speak, were somewhat more disposed to hear me out.

I have always had confidence in my abilities to dominate any adversary when it comes to a discussion. I don't know whether by force of logic or some natural talent, the truth is, while alive, I could always win any debate dependent upon irrefutably solid argumentation.

Death had not impaired this capacity. And my murderers did me justice. After a short debate, in which I explained with great clarity my own views, the fellows felt completely at a loss to find any solution that would attend, satisfactorily, as much to my reasoning as to their own program for the evening, still to be continued. But to make things even more confusing, they sensed the futility of giving any direction to a deceased who had yet to lose any of those faculties generally attributed to the living.

Had a suggestion not occurred finally to one of their group and been adopted immediately, we would have remained at an impasse. The fellow proposed including me in the group, so that, together, we might finish out the evening that had been interrupted by my being run over.

In the meantime, another obstacle intervened: there were only three girls, which is to say, a number equal to the boys. One for me was still missing, and I refused to join them while still unaccompanied myself. The same fellow, however, who had proposed my inclusion in the group came up with the perfect conciliatory solution by suggesting they abandon the friend who had passed out on the road just before. To improve my appearance, he added, it would be enough merely to switch my clothes with the ones Jorge was wearing, something I declared myself ready to do on the spot.

Beyond a certain reluctance to abandon their colleague like that, everyone (both male and female, the latter now recovered from the early fainting) agreed that he had been weak and had not known how to confront the situation with dignity, therefore it was hardly reasonable for us to waste further time with sentimental reflections upon his person.

Of what happened afterward I retain no very clear recollection. The drinking, which before my death had always affected me very little, suddenly produced surprising effects upon my now defunct person. Stars entered through my eyes, and lights whose colors were unknown to me, then absurd triangles, ivory cones and spheres, black roses, carnations shaped like lilies, lilies transformed into hands. And the redhead, who had been allotted me by the group, suddenly squeezed me around the neck with her body, which had somehow been transformed into one long metallic arm.

With the coming of daylight, I was roused from my semilethargic state. Someone asked me where I wished to be dropped off. I remember I insisted on getting out at the cemetery, which they replied was impossible, since at that hour it would certainly be closed. I repeated several times the word *cemetery*. (Who knows whether I managed actually to repeat it, or only moved my lips, trying to link words to the remote sensations of my polychromatic delirium.)

For a considerable time afterward I continued to suffer from the disequilibrium between the exterior world and my eyes, which refused to adjust to the bright color of the landscapes stretching before me, and from the fear that would persist from that morning when I first discovered that death had penetrated my body.

If it weren't for the skepticism of men refusing to accept me alive or dead, I might have taken heart in my ambition to construct a new existence.

I've still had to fight constantly against that madness which, at times, becomes master of my actions and compels me to search anxiously in all the daily papers for any news that might somehow elucidate the mystery still surrounding my decease.

I made various attempts to establish contact with my companions of the fatal night in question, but the results were equally discouraging. And there lay my only hope to prove the real extent of my death.

As the months passed, my suffering became less acute, and my frustration less extreme, at the difficulty of convincing friends that the Zacarias who walks the city streets is the same pyrotechnical artist of times gone by, with the single difference that the other was alive, while this one is a corpse.

Only one thought really troubles me: what events will fate hold in store for a dead man, if the living breathe such agonizing lives? And my anxiety increases on sensing, in all its fullness, how my capacity to love, to discern things, is far superior to that of the many who pass me by so fearfully.

Still, a clear day might dawn tomorrow, the sun brilliant as never before. And at such an hour men may come to realize that, even on the margin of life, I am still alive, because my existence has been transmuted into colors, and whiteness is already drawing close to the earth, to the exclusive delight of my eyes.

The City

The labor of the foolish
wearieth every one of them,
because he knoweth not how
to go to the city.
                    Ecclesiastes, x:15

He was headed for a larger city when the train stalled, indefinitely, at the penultimate station.

Cariba imagined that the delay was most likely attributable to the derailment of some freight train, a fairly common occurrence along this stretch of the tracks. Still, the wait did seem excessive, and since no one had bothered to come and explain to him what was going on, he began to suspect a possible lack of consideration: the fact of his being the only passenger aboard the train.

He summoned the conductor who had originally punched his ticket, to inquire if the emptiness of the coach had, in point of fact, merited such a degree of neglect.

No direct answer was given by the railroad employee. He simply pointed to the nearby hill, which was spotted haphazardly by dozens of little white cottages.

"Beautiful women, eh?" The traveler smiled.

"Empty houses."

Cariba understood immediately that the man was a cretin, so he picked up his luggage and prepared to climb the sheer slopes that would take him to the village.

The ascent was slow and tiresome. Perspiration beaded his forehead, while his eyes were magnetized by the delicacy of those tiny, cabana-like constructions.

A vague sadness seemed to permeate the little hamlet. The doors and windows of the houses were locked shut, yet the gardens appeared to have been recently watered. He tried knocking at some doors, but no one answered anywhere. So he climbed still higher and from there, on the summit of the mountain, caught a first glimpse of the entire city, as large as that city he had been destined for: more than twenty thousand inhabitants, he found out later.

Sluggishly, he descended. The men (and why not the beautiful ladies?) ought to be somewhere down below.

Several times he had to glance over his shoulder, trying to fix in his mind an image of the landscape receding behind him. He had an impression it was unlikely he would return that way.

For the remainder of the journey—from secondary roads down to the main thoroughfare—inhabitants of the area eyed Cariba suspiciously. Perhaps they were put off by his camel-hide luggage, or the checkered jacket he was wearing, with blue corduroy pants. Though it was quite normal attire for his constant travels, he thought it prudent to avoid any misunderstanding that could be provoked by his appearance:

"What city might this be?" he inquired, trying to lend his words the tone of utmost cordiality.

There was no chance to address himself to the ladies, the way he might have intended. He was violently seized by the arms and dragged roughly away to police headquarters.

"Here's the one you're after," they announced to the desk officer, a stocky, brutish sergeant.

"We've got plenty of drifters around these parts already," he growled. "What did you come here for?"

"Nothing."

"Then it's you, all right. I never heard of anybody going to some city they don't know without any reason. Unless it's a tourist . . . "

"I'm not a tourist, and I want to know where I am."

"That we can't tell you just yet. It would prejudice our investigation."

"And why were those houses up on the hill all closed up?" the traveler interrupted, annoyed at the lack of courtesy in the way he was being treated.

"If we didn't take that precaution, you probably wouldn't have come down here."

Cariba realized too late: the seductiveness of the white houses had been merely a stratagem to attract him to the valley below.

"The witnesses!" shouted the officer.

A skinny-faced, gray-haired fellow was brought in. He politely bowed to the sergeant, and then turned to the prisoner with visible repugnance:

"I'm not afraid to face you."

"We're not interested in your courage, for the moment," the sergeant cut in sharply. "Just stick to the question put to you and answer whether you recognize this man."

"No. I never saw him before, but I have the feeling he was the one who came up to me on the street. He asked me questions about our local customs and then disappeared."

The officer grew impatient:

"Bring in the other idiots!"

One after another, various people testified, but without

shedding light on the matter. With some the stranger had apparently raised issues of minor import: "Is this city new or old?" With others, however, his questioning was more impertinent: "Who runs this town, anyway?"

A number of witnesses had actually seen the suspect face to face, but without his having uttered a word to them. On only one point were all in agreement, whether they had been lucky enough to have heard his voice or had merely caught a glimpse of his face: none knew how to describe his physical appearance, if he was tall or short, the color of his skin, or what language he had spoken.

The last of them had already been dismissed when the officer triumphantly banged his fist down on the table:

"Bring Viegas here, she knows!"

Two hours went by before the girl arrived. She sauntered in unembarrassedly, her lips slightly frosted, her eyebrows tweezed, and a smile on her face that left Cariba enchanted.

Enraptured by the charms of the prostitute, who, for her part, kept her eyes fixed on his, the poor foreigner hardly picked up a word she said. Little by little, he found his way back to reality, though, and slowly began to pay attention to her testimony.

"I tried to run, but he grabbed me by the wrists and asked: 'How is your father? Still living with those spinster aunts?' Not getting any response, he went on to question me about my children. You know well enough, Sergeant, that I'm single, and that Father was living by himself when he died. That's why, even before he finished questioning me, I'd already come to suspect him, and struggled to wrench myself from his hands. I couldn't, though. He gripped me even more tightly and, forcing me to rest my ear against his lips, he whispered: 'It's good to conspire.' In hopes of convincing him to go away, I tried to point out the dangers to which he was exposed, confronting a police force as tough as ours. Showing no fear, he answered me: 'The police won't be necessary.' "

Cariba felt a great deal of envy for the one who had actually embraced that woman. What a body to have held in your arms!

The police sergeant, however, was not content with what he had heard:

"And you recognize this man as the one who grabbed you out on the street?"

"I don't remember his face exactly, but they're one and the same person, all right."

The officer was satisfied now. He turned to the accused to indicate that, even though he had enough evidence at this point to close the case, he would hear the witnesses once again in his presence, which he in fact now proceeded to do with his customary lack of civility:

"So you idiots mean to tell me that you actually saw his face and yet don't know how to describe him?"

With the exception of Viegas, all remained silent. She, on the other hand, fixing her eyes maliciously upon the defendant, now swore:

"Yes, it's him!"

The sergeant had clearly reached a decision, but hesitated:

"The telegram from the Chief of Police makes no reference to the nationality of the suspect in question, to his age, his appearance, or even the crimes he committed. It simply states that we're dealing with a highly dangerous individual who may be identified by the habit of asking questions, and we should expect him to be arriving sometime today."

Cariba, already uncomfortable at the prospect of remaining in custody until the whole mix-up could be straightened out, suddenly muttered aloud:

"None of this makes any sense. They can't just arrest me on the basis of what I've heard so far. I only arrived a few hours ago, for the first time, and these witnesses claim to have seen me as far back as a week ago!"

The officer prevented him from continuing any further:

"The communication from our security section is clear enough, and states as follows: 'The man will arrive on the fifteenth,' which is today, 'and can be recognized by his exaggerated curiosity.'"

The police sergeant now formally closed the inquiry, declaring that those depositions hitherto rendered were sufficient testimony to charge the accused. However, he would still refrain from acting precipitously. Instead, he preferred to await the appearance of someone who might exhibit greater signs of culpability, and thereby exonerate Cariba of the charges weighing against him.

"Which is to say, in the meantime I must remain a prisoner?"

The officer's answer crushed him: he would be detained until such time as the real criminal was apprehended.

And what if the guilty party doesn't exist?

After five long months of incarceration Cariba no longer has hopes of a reprieve. From behind bars he continually observes the people who go by on the street. But they hardly look at him; they hurry past, frightened.

At times he gets the feeling they must be on the verge of

asking a question. He watches them carefully, anxious for that to happen. Yet disappointment quickly sets in again. They open their mouths for a second, but change their minds and depart abruptly.

The women, quite fearless, habitually drop by the station to offer cigarettes. They seem so beautiful, exactly like the ones he had hoped to find in that distant metropolis. Shy and wordless, they note the desperation in his eyes—of not holding them close or feeling their warm breath.

He can only wait for Viegas, who visits him every evening, sensual and perfumed. She smiles, and whispers with almost touching predictability:

"I know it's you."

When she leaves, Cariba—his body tensed, the sweat pouring from his temples—once again realizes the immense power of that imprisonment.

He'll pace back and forth during the night, but whenever he sees the guard making his nocturnal rounds to ascertain all is in order, he leaps at the bars of his cell, driven by some vague expectation:

"Has anyone asked any questions today?"

"No, you're still the only one to ask questions in the city."

Marina,
the Intangible

Who is she that looketh forth
as the morning, fair as the moon,
clear as the sun, and terrible
as an army with banners?
The Song of Solomon VI:10

There was no time to cry for help as silence engulfed me.
Total silence: not even the sound of my heartbeat. I set
down the Bible, and readied myself for whatever might
happen. Surely it must be the advent of Marina.

Agonized by the absence of noises in the room, I got up
from my chair, wanting to flee. I had hardly moved, though,
before I sat down again: nothing could dispel such emptiness as now permeated the morning. Sounds would have to
begin elsewhere.

Finally, two chimes reverberated, long and heavy. The
stillness in the air augmented their volume and clarity—
intensifying my dark forebodings. They originated from
the Capuchin chapel, at whose steps I always genuflected
on my way to work at the newspaper.

Since my helplessness seemed to persist, I stammered
out a prayer to Marina, the Intangible. The praying helped
to quell my anxiety, yet it did little to rid me of an inability
to face the night's work.

Unimpressed by the fact that the chapel actually possessed no clock, I pressed my temples with my fingers,

trying to concentrate upon present obligations. However, the wastebasket full of crumpled paper discouraged me.

I shifted restlessly in my chair, staring impotently at the white sheets of paper where I had already scribbled a few disconnected phrases. Except for a sensation of absolute futility, my brain was empty, and I had no hope of someone to help me.

In order to vanquish my sterility somehow, I attacked the page before me, disposed to write any sort of story, even the most chaotic and absurd. My desperation, however, only added to the difficulty of expressing myself. Whenever sentences did come easily, filling several sheets of paper, I would realize almost immediately that a subject was lacking. I seemed to be writing incoherencies.

So I began inventing various excuses to explain my unexpected inhibitions. I blamed the morning's silence, the lack of any close colleague. I failed, however, to convince myself: what about other days? I was simply the only journalist assigned to the night shift. Since it was an evening paper, quite logically the editorial staff was restricted to the morning hours.

I even tried to persuade myself that, whether or not I wrote, the result would be the same. The editor-in-chief never used my articles or my chronicles for the morning edition, nor specified the actual assignments I ought to be undertaking instead. In order to make up for such a disagreeable omission, my only option was to invent material, by poring anxiously over old papers, which I could use in my stories. I had already broached, in long articles, the smallest details regarding the distance I covered, normally, between my house and the office, without neglecting to describe (tenderly) our own garden. A tiny garden in the shape of a half-moon, with rosebushes and dried-out daisies.

Long before hearing the dull murmur of the chimes, I was already unnerved by my growing presentiments. The idea of waiting seemed intolerable. Let whatever threatened to be, arise! At any moment, I imagined, I could be thrown out of my chair and hurled into the air. The action of gravity was about to be broken.

Again I opened the Bible. Less disturbed now. The silence had been dispelled, and—in spite of my knowing that the hours were being marked by an invisible clock—I felt certain that time had recovered its normal rhythm. (That was important to me, not wanting to remain frozen somewhere in time.)

After leafing through a few pages, I finally discovered the subject I was searching for. I wanted to write about the mystery of Marina, the Intangible—also known as Maria da Conceição. (She had changed her name after fleeing from Nova Lima, along with her lover. She never actually loved him. They say that he, an old soldier, carried hundreds of scars on his chest from numerous revolutions, but still was never promoted.

My happiness at having so easily encountered the phrase to open my essay was not to last very long. As I started to write it down, it fled from my pen.

I opened the window which looked out onto the garden, in order to catch the scent of the roses. Perhaps they would help me.

Upon lifting the venetian blind, however, I noticed the face of a stranger. Quickly, I averted my eyes. The face made me uncomfortable: the whole of it occupied by a gross, hooked nose. I took another look at the intruder and saw that he was staring right back at me.

Without altering his facial expression, or moving so much as a muscle, he announced to me:

"I got your message, José Ambrósio, so here I am."

I was quite paralyzed as I contemplated his motionless face, the disproportionate head which filled a good part of the window.

Recovering from the shock caused by such a presence, I responded vigorously:

"I don't know you, and I have no time to bother with you right now."

Then I motioned him to go away. His figure, so awkward and strange, somehow tormented me, preventing me from elaborating my proposed text.

I think he mistook my gesture as an invitation to come inside, since he merely walked the few steps necessary to come to the front door and enter the living room.

Pausing only a few feet from my desk, he continued staring at me. Such a frail body, dressed in ordinary clothes; such an immense nose, with those placid features. (A new idea came to mind, yet I refused to allow it to materialize, intuiting somehow that he would never permit it to be carried out.)

Realizing, moreover, that on that morning none of my obligations were about to be met with, I pushed aside my papers and prepared myself to hear him out.

"It's the poem needed for publication. The one you asked me for."

"I've never asked you for anything. Please go away, I have more urgent business to attend to."

"You did ask. Perhaps you no longer remember, because the request you made was prior to your illness."

I lost control, hearing such an idiotic statement. Me, sick? Still, better to close the matter, once and for all, and end the discussion:

"Any poetic form goes beyond the scope of the paper. Especially if not even my articles, which are far more important, ever get published!"

Upset enough already, not to be further irritated by this incomprehensible fellow, I leaped from my chair, shouting:

"Death to poetry, death to poets!"

I advanced upon him furiously, with the intention of grabbing him by the neck. At least I would kill this poet.

He was slowly backing away, his face impassive, without the slightest fear of my threatening posture. And as I approached him now, he cautiously retreated until his back touched the wall behind him. Suddenly recoiling, he made one last attempt to move me:

"It's a poem to Marina, the Intangible."

I fell to my knees.

We had to publish the poem. But how? I rested my hand amicably upon his shoulder and explained to the poet once again that my superiors had discarded everything which, with such painstaking elaboration, I had written each previous night.

He seemed not to attribute any importance to my explanation and said it was our job to eliminate whatever obstacles we might encounter. Since there was so little interest in publishing it, we should undertake to do it ourselves: a special evening edition totally dedicated to Marina.

"And the staff to compose and print such an edition?" I asked him.

"That part of the job will also be left to us."

I thought the idea was a rather good one, except for my knowing that the paper had no Linotype machines, no printing presses, and I, no knowledge of typesetting.

In order to gain time, I asked him to show me his verses.

"I don't have them with me, or anywhere else."

"But how can we print them if they don't exist?"

"You have to write them."

"But if I can only do Biblical poems?"

"That's exactly what I want. Marina's existence is contained in a passage from the Song of Songs: 'I charge you, O daughters of Jerusalem, if ye find my beloved, that ye tell him, that I am sick with love.' "

"Even so, I have no idea how to write it."

"Just keep looking at me and write," he commanded.

And he began to make signs with his hands. Slow gestures which, rhythmically, first concealed and then revealed his placid, immobile face.

I was unable to translate all the movements, yet—strangely—I felt the poem of Marina was about to be born! With lovely, invisible verses!

"It's finished," he declared with conviction. "Now, simply do the typesetting."

I looked at the sheet of paper without a line written upon it, yet did not have the courage to contradict him. Instead, I followed him farther inside, toward the back of the house.

We went through a number of doorways. I was walking slowly with the blank page in hand, meditating some way to demonstrate to him the impossibility of editing a special edition of the paper.

As we entered the old kitchen, the last room in the house, with access to the backyard, I gave my companion a push from behind and shouted:

"It's ridiculous to go any farther. We have no offices here, and this piece of paper is an odious mystification!"

"Marina's verses have no need of machinery," he answered, pulling me along.

My capacity to resist was depleted. In silence, I accompanied him out to the yard.

"Bring me those roses," he ordered as soon as we were near the fence.

Too powerless to formulate an objection gnawing at my insides, I picked the roses and brought them back to him. I was done for. Not even my roses, which had never been picked and lost their petals only with the passage of time, escaped the virulence of the stranger. And I, so weakly, surrendered to his caprices.

He stripped the flowers of their petals with slow deliberation, totally absorbed in his task. He tore each petal in half and placed them all on the ground. He formed words I was unable to decipher and then, in a low voice, concluded:

"The first songs are made from apetalous roses: recalling Paradise before the Fall."

"And the last?" I said, afflicted.

"Nonexistent," he answered, as he continued strewing petals.

They could never stop existing, I thought to myself with anguish.

Far from feeling my own anxiety, the poet bent over his task. After some time had elapsed, he murmured:

"Only the sunflower is lacking."

I perceived that the moment for definitive action had arrived. (First there had been the roses, untouched by anyone. And now the sunflowers, which were nonexistent and could hardly be stripped of their petals!) I rushed at him, prepared to tear him apart. Without backing away, he raised his short and fleshless arms on high: bells chimed, solemn and measured.

The Capuchin fathers appeared. Briskly, they scaled the wall, blowing silent trumpets. (Ten walls they scaled, and ten were still to come.) A little behind them marched the Fleur-de-Lys Philharmonica, with cornetists in green uniforms. They were playing their instruments separately and without music. Simply blowing them. They filled the night with piercing sounds, savage and cacophonic.

A chorus of men with withered faces followed. The principals stretched open their mouths as if they desired to sing, but emitted no sounds. One of them, dressed as a sexton, carried the clock from the Capuchin chapel.

I had no opportunity to rejoice at verifying its existence, because there, on a litter decorated with crepe paper, Marina appeared, the Intangible One, escorted by freckled priests and pregnant women. She was wearing a dress of crushed satin, the hem of which was stained with mud. On her head, a felt hat, rather faded-looking, sporting a chicken feather. Her lips were excessively painted, and the eyes, in heavy shadow done with black charcoal. In her right hand she held a sunflower, and she gazed upon me with tenderness. Under the torn dress I glimpsed her white, shapely thighs. I hesitated an instant between her eyes and her legs. But, suddenly, metallic angels blocked my view, while their figures began to enlarge and diminish rapidly.

They swiftly passed, vaulting over walls which surfaced continuously as various planes rose and fell. I ran from one extreme to the other, panting, exhausted, now seeking her eyes, now searching out the thighs of Marina, until typographers brought up the rear of the procession. Linotypes came flying along, and Linotype operators, busy setting type, concentrated on their labors. Then the typeface, in script and italic . . . And the printers, walking on long wooden stilts, filling the yard with papers.

In a matter of seconds the procession was finished, and the walls which had risen before me a moment before merged into the single wall. I wanted to run, to overtake the litter that bore Marina, but all the newspapers, which had been tossed in the air and strewn on the ground, now made me stumble.

When I finally got disentangled, I found myself alone in the garden, and no sound, no noise whatsoever, could be heard. I realized, nonetheless, that Marina's poem had somehow been composed, irrevocably so. Fashioned of torn petals and dumb sounds . . .

The Ex-Magician from the Minhota Tavern

*Bow down thine ear, O Lord, and
hear me: for I am poor and needy.*
Psalms, LXXXVI:1

Nowadays I'm a civil servant, which is not my greatest misfortune.

To be honest, I was not prepared for suffering. Each man, on reaching a certain age, is perfectly equipped to face the avalanche of tedium and bitterness, since from his early childhood he has become accustomed to the vicissitudes of daily life through a gradual process of continual vexation.

This did not happen to me. I was cast into existence without parents, without infancy or adolescence.

I found myself one day, with light gray hair, in the mirror of the Minhota Tavern, a discovery which in no way frightened me, any more than it astonished me to take the owner of the restaurant out of my pocket. He, rather perplexed, asked me how could I have done such a thing.

What could I answer, given my situation, a person who lacked the least explanation for his presence in the world? I said to him that I was tired, that I was born tired and weary.

Without weighing my answer or questioning me any further, he made me an offer of a job, and so I began, from that time on, to entertain the clientele of the establishment with my magical activity.

The man himself, however, failed to appreciate my habit of offering onlookers a variety of free lunches, which I would mysteriously draw forth from the inside of my own jacket. Judging it to be not the best of transactions merely to increase the number of customers—without a corresponding growth in profits—he introduced me to the impresario of the Andalusian Circus Garden, who, when told of my aptitudes, offered to hire me. First, however, he was advised to take certain precautions over my tricks, since I might just decide to distribute free admissions to the performances.

Contrary to the pessimistic expectations of my first employer, my behavior was exemplary. My public engagements not only thrilled multitudes, but brought in fabulous profits for the company owners as well.

Audiences, in general, received me rather coolly, perhaps because I failed to present myself in tails and a top hat. But as soon as I began involuntarily to extract rabbits, snakes, lizards from a hat, spectators tingled with excitement, above all in the last number, when I would cause an alligator to appear from the tips of my fingers. Then, by compressing the animal from both ends, I changed him into an accordion and brought the act to its close by playing the Cochin China National Anthem. Applause would burst forth from all sides, under my remote gaze.

The manager of the circus, observing me from a distance, was exasperated by my indifference to the public's acclaim, especially when it came from the younger children who would show up to clap for me at Sunday matinees.

Why be moved, though, if those innocent faces, destined to endure the suffering inflicted upon any man's coming of age, aroused no pity in me, much less any anger, over their having everything I longed for but did not myself possess: birth, and a past.

As I grew more popular, my life became intolerable.

At times, sitting in some café, stubbornly observing the populace filing past on the sidewalks, I would end up pulling doves, gulls, skunks out of my pocket. The people around me, judging my behavior to be intentional, invariably broke into shrill peals of laughter. I would stare at the floor dejectedly, and mutter against the world and birds.

Whenever, absentmindedly, I happened to open my hands, curious objects slid out of them. On a certain occasion I surprised myself by pulling one shape after another out of my sleeve. In the end I was completely surrounded by strange shapes, without any idea of what purpose to attribute to them.

What could I do? I looked all around me, my eyes pleading for some kind of help, in vain, an excruciating state of affairs.

Almost always, if I took out my handkerchief to blow my nose, I astonished those nearby by pulling a whole bedsheet out of my pocket. If I fidgeted with the collar of my coat, a large buzzard would immediately appear. On other occasions, while trying to tie my shoelaces, snakes would slither out of my trousers. Women and children started screaming. Guards came over, bystanders crowding around, a scandal. I would have to report to police headquarters and listen patiently while I was prohibited by the authorities from any further setting loose of serpents on public thoroughfares.

I raised no objection. Timid, I humbly mentioned my condition of magician, reaffirmed my intention not to bother anyone.

I became accustomed, at night, to waking up quite suddenly in the middle of a sound sleep, with a loud bird flapping its wings as it took flight from my ear.

On one of these occasions, completely furious, and resolved never again to practice magic, I cut off my hands. To no purpose. As soon as I moved, they reappeared, fresh and perfect, on the ends of the stump of each arm!

I had to resolve my despair somehow. After weighing the matter carefully, I concluded that only death would put a proper end to my misfortune.

Steadfast in my decision, I took a dozen lions out of my pockets and, crossing my arms, waited for the moment when I would be devoured. They did me no harm. Surrounding me, they sniffed at my clothes and, eyeing the landscape, slunk away.

Next morning they were back again and sat themselves provocatively before me.

"What do you expect from me, stupid animals?" I roared indignantly.

They shook their manes sadly and pleaded with me to make them disappear.

"This world is tremendously tedious," they declared.

I failed to restrain my outright rage. I killed them all, and began to devour them myself. I had hopes of dying the victim of a fatal indigestion.

Misfortune of misfortunes! I suffered an enormous stomachache, and continued to live.

This failure only multiplied my sense of frustration. I left the city limits and went off in search of the mountains. Reaching the highest peak, which dominated the dark abyss, I relinquished my body to space.

I felt no more than a slight sensation of the closeness of death—almost at once I found myself suspended from a parachute. With difficulty, battering myself against rocks, maimed and grimy, I finally returned to the city, where my first step was to acquire a pistol.

At home again and lying on my bed, I raised the weapon to my ear. I pulled the trigger, expecting a loud report and the pain of the bullet tearing through my head.

There was no shot, and no death: the handgun turned into a pencil.

I rolled to the floor, sobbing. I who could create other beings had no means to liberate myself from existence.

An expression I overheard by accident, out on the street one day, brought me renewed hope of a definitive break with life. From a sad man I heard that to be a civil servant was to commit suicide little by little.

I was in no condition to determine which form of suicide was best suited to me: slow or quick. As a result, I took a job in the Department of State.

1930, a bitter year, longer than those that followed the first manifestation I had of my existence, back in the mirror at the Minhota Tavern.

I did not die, as I had hoped to. The greater my afflictions were, the greater my misfortune.

While I was a magician, I had had very little to do with people—the stage always kept me at a comfortable distance. Now that I was obliged to have constant contact with my fellow creatures, it was necessary to understand them, and to disguise the repugnance they aroused in me.

The worst of it was that, my duties being rather trivial, I found myself in the position of having to hang around uselessly for hours at a stretch. Idleness led to my resenting the lack of a past. Why was it only me, among all those existing before my very eyes, who had nothing to recall? My days floated in confusion, mixed with a few paltry recollections, the small plus of three years in existence.

Love, which came to me by way of another civil servant, her desk close to mine, distracted me for a time from my worries.

Momentary distraction. My restlessness quickly returned, I struggled with uncertainties. How was I to propose to this colleague of mine if I had never made declarations of love, nor had a single amorous experience?

1931 began cheerlessly, with threats of mass dismissals in our department and a refusal by the typist to consider my proposal. Faced with the possibility of being discharged, I tried somehow to look after my own interests. (The job mattered little to me. I was simply afraid of leaving behind a woman by whom I had been rejected, but whose presence slowly became indispensable to me.)

I went to the supervisor of our section and announced that I could not be fired because, after ten years in the department, I now possessed job security.

He stared at me for some time in total silence. Then,

frowning at me, he said he was astonished by my cynicism. He would never have expected anyone with only one year of service to have the audacity to claim ten.

To prove to him that my attitude was not frivolous, I rummaged through my pockets for some documents corroborating the authenticity of my claim. Stunned, I managed to pull out only a crumpled piece of paper, the fragment of a poem inspired by the breasts of the typist.

Anxiously, I turned all my pockets inside out, but found nothing more. . . .

I was forced to admit defeat. I had trusted too much in my powers to make magic, which had been nullified by bureaucracy.

Nowadays, without the aforementioned and miraculous gift of wizardry, I am unable to relinquish the very worst of human occupations. I lack the love of my typist companion and the presence of friends, which obliges me to frequent solitary places. I am often caught attempting to remove, from the inside of my clothes with my fingers, little things which no one glimpses anyway, no matter how attentively they gaze.

They think that I'm crazy, chiefly when I toss into the air those tiny objects.

I have the impression that a swallow is about to disengage itself from my fingertips. I sigh aloud, deeply.

Of course, the illusion gives me no comfort. It only serves to intensify my regret not to have created a total magical world.

At certain moments I imagine how marvelous it would be to extract red, blue, white, and green handkerchiefs from my body, fill the night with fireworks, turn my face to the sky and let a rainbow pour forth from my lips, a rainbow that could cover the earth from one extremity to the other. Then the applause from the old men with their white hair, and from gentle children.

Mariazinha

Thy silver is become dross,
thy wine mixed with water.
Isaiah, 1:22

1943

"Josefino Maria Albuquerque Pereira da Silva!" The voice came in slow, lugubrious, declamatory fashion. The words traced curves through the air and invaded my ear like drops of oil, penetrating sluggishly, losing the Silva. The last name was left out. And the oil was heavy.

My mind wandered: the names wavered indolently, merging together, hoping to make room for the Silva waiting in the vestibule.

I lifted my head and stared straight before me, then to the side. The space danced around me, changed its planes, until finally I managed to distinguish the monotonous figure of Father Delfim, who, seated on the edge of the bed, had his eyes focused on my forehead. I repeatedly moved my lips, imploring him to leave me in peace. The effort got lost somewhere in the void, and I couldn't hear my own calling.

Then there were some Latin phrases.

My brother was also in the room. Mournfully, he hid in

his hands the silhouette of Mariazinha. (The cigarette had made me nauseous and the liquor dizzy, but I never heard the actual report. I had resolutely gripped the revolver, aimed at a black spot which was projected from my eyes and which, in the air, accompanied the rhythm of my pupils. Bells tolled.)

It must have been the bullet that wouldn't permit the Silva to enter.

The clapper in the largest bell struck the other bells: some bronze, others of tin and zinc. The music sounded harsh, mortifying—cries of the dead and the dying.

1923

May somersaulted—an unhappy month, when I first met Mariazinha and listened to her story—stretching its whole self out before me, accommodating all the years that had passed, giving me back my hair and Mariazinha her virginity.

Everything recommenced for the inhabitants of Manacá. There were some protests, since many of them refused to accept the loss of the children, returned to their mothers' wombs, or the absence of pavement on the streets. But the excessive dust on public thoroughfares hardly affected the rejoicing of others who, with the sudden change in civil status, became single once again. (And swore never to re-marry.)

Father Delfim was to become bishop. Now the bells ought to sound happy, to forget the dead. Their sadness, however, was oppressive, and muted them. The sexton had lost his job.

D. Delfim had an insipid face and a calm disposition. He ordered steel chimes to be found, metal instruments, and prohibited further melancholy, or complaints regarding the dusty streets.

Mariazinha was to be married. Her seducer would be hanged from the belfry tower.

The bells applauded, tinkling joyfully, but D. Delfim's face reddened and lost its monotonous expression. He ordered away the steel chimes, the metal instruments.

Zaragota protested:

"You won't hang me!" It was all right to kill him before, when he had seduced Mariazinha, but not now. Twenty years had elapsed. He was no longer anyone's fiancé, or even a member of the eminent bishop's diocese.

D. Delfim stroked his chin, pleased with the adjective and the scent of perfume emanating from his white lace handkerchief.

All he could think of was the upcoming celebration to commemorate his elevation to bishop, fearful that some unpredictable event might rob some of the splendor from the tribute he was to receive.

Meanwhile, he had to give the people a little more cause for rejoicing. He was adamant. His right to be eminent was something no one was going to deny him. He lifted his head, haughty, energetic, and ordered:

"Josefino Maria Albuquerque Pereira da Silva, you must hang the man!"

Afterward, lending his expression an air of tenderness and (ecclesiastical) humility, he told me: "You must ring the bells and wed Mariazinha."

Since no one dissented, the scoundrel Zaragota was executed, and preparations were begun for my wedding.

The first thing to be taken care of was the gown for my bride. We all agreed it shouldn't be long, with a train, although no one dared to mention the reason. (D. Delfim never threatened twice. Any reference to dust on the streets was, therefore, carefully omitted.)

Mariazinha, restless and overjoyed to be suddenly fifteen again, had no objections to anything. She just grabbed me by the hand and dragged me off on long walks with her. We would leave the town far behind us and run along country roads, cutting through forests, climbing over peaks. She skipped along, loading me with flowers and kisses. At the same time Manacá busily spruced itself up. Triumphal arches and banners of crepe paper were being hung across the streets, while church bells rang and D. Delfim hurriedly passed by in his carriage to inspect it all, his baldness protected by an enormous leather cap.

On the day marked for our nuptials, the city dawned in a flurry. (Zaragota swung from the belfry tower.)

The whole town had gathered, by the early morning hours, there in front of the church. José Alfinete commanded the populace from the middle of the plaza. For more than an hour he'd been spewing out his inflammatory rhetoric, analyzing the chaotic state of the nation, the farm crisis, and the problems with the pharmacist, his political opponent.

Were it not for the orator, who had actually convoked the people of Manacá to confide the terrible news, no one would have known the reason for the gathering. Two hours after beginning his speech Alfinete revealed that Mariazinha had been seduced again and the seducer had fled.

The citizenry, outraged by what they had just heard, banded together in hot pursuit, disposed to hang me in the public square.

When my pursuers finally caught up with me, it was relatively late for them to think of executing me. I had already fired at the black spot which, in the air, accompanied the movement of my pupils, so I was stretched out, face down, on the ground.

The evening before, contrary to what they had so cunningly announced, it was I who was seduced by Mariazinha.

On returning to town, I had no further doubts that my bride-to-be was completely depraved. Poor Zaragota had not been to blame.

I couldn't get to sleep that night. Alarmed by what had happened, I decided not to marry. I left the house and went drinking in all the taverns I could find along the way. I wanted to drown myself in alcohol.

Much later I retraced our walk of the previous evening.

I paused in the same spot where I had lain with Mariazinha. The stars sank into my eyes and the black spot stood out clearly in the moonlight. I softly pulled the trigger.

The bells of Manacá were sad all over again. D. Delfim saw himself deprived of all his episcopal honors.

1943

"Josefino Maria Albuquerque Pereira da Silva!"

The voice was slow, lugubrious, declamatory. Father Delfim called me in vain.

The streets of the city now displayed their former pavements, and the sons of its inhabitants began to exit—without the need of assistance from midwives—from the wombs of their mothers. Manacá was once more elevated to the status of county seat, and the men who had sworn never to remarry had sworn to no avail.

Zaragota, faithful friend, would show up at my funeral, still convalescing from the hanging he had endured.

Actually, he didn't show up. Father Delfim still judged him to be the cause of his demission and, as a consolation, ordered him to be hanged from the same spot as the previous time.

The bells tolled, sad and cracked. The sexton had been rehired. For several nights the moon flooded the dustless streets of the city, and May slowly drew to a close.